LUNA STATION
QUARTERLY

ISSUE 021
MARCH 2015

EDITOR & PUBLISHER
Jennifer Lyn Parsons

ASSISTANT EDITORS
Tara Calaby
Cathrin Hagey
Andi Marquette
Megan Patton
Danielle Perry
Iona Sharma

COVER ARTIST
Erin DeMoss

LUNA STATION PRESS

First Paperback Edition March 2015

ISBN: 978-1-938697-57-9

Luna Station Quarterly publishes short fiction on March 1st, June 1st, September 1st, and December 1st. For more information and submission guidelines, please visit our website at lunastationquarterly.com

For Luna Station Press

Creative Director - Tara Quinn Lindsey

LUNA STATION PRESS

576 Valley Road #197

Wayne, NJ 07470

www.lunastationpress.com

info@lunastationpress.com

CONTENTS

EDITORIAL
JENNIFER LYN PARSONS

Even though the future seems far away,
it is actually beginning right now.

~ Mattie Stepanek

Five years down and the future is yet ahead. And, as the quote above says, it's starting right now.

This issue, the one you are reading now, marks the beginning of Luna Station Quarterly's sixth year. I will save my thoughts on the last five years. You'll be able to see them when our first anthology comes out next month. (from Luna Station Press, see the last page for details!!!)

Instead I'll talk about the future.

The most important thing about this issue is that it is possible you are holding our first print edition in your hands. When the first proof came in, I was elated. To be able to see these marvelous stories in print felt like such a landmark in my journey with LSQ.

It's thanks to the developments in digital printing that I'm finally able to make this dream a reality. And I'm not stopping here. The rest of the issues this year will be available in print as well. Additionally, I'll be releasing omnibus editions of the last five years through Luna Station Press. After that, single editions of all of the back issues.

LSQ fully and perpetually in print. I could swoon.

I hope you all noticed our new design, too! After many years with the same look, it was time to give LSQ a shot in the arm. Alongside the new interiors, this year will feature cover illustrations by the talented Erin DeMoss who'll be focussing on famous female genre fiction authors.

An all new style for the issues pushes me towards another project on the docket: a new website.

The new site (besides being easier for the staff to use) will have an entirely new design that I think you are all going to love. I'll be sure to put the word out when it goes live later this year.

I also want to take a moment and look forward beyond the borders of LSQ.

Women are making a move. Momentum towards real change is building so rapidly it makes my head spin.

Tolerance is rapidly diminishing for places where more than half of the human population is not considered equal. Geek girls know they have every right to enjoy the games, comics, and other media that they love and defy the 'that's for boys' label that gets slapped on so much pop culture.

As a web developer, I take pride in the work I do and connecting with other women in my field and I'm finding that things are shifting. Even in places that are still male-dominated, women are being measured by the quality of their work.

And the changes keep on coming and I couldn't be happier.

If the time ever comes when there is not a 'need' for places like Luna Station Quarterly, I'll be thrilled. But even when that future comes into being, there will always be a place here for women who simply want to share a supportive community, for new writers to find their feet, and for us all to share marvelous tales of wonder, exploration, and what it is that makes us all human.

LSQ·021

THE GOLD FISH
KIM MARY TROTTO

Kim Mary Trotto is a retired journalist. She has short stories published on several Webzine sites and features and essays published in various New Jersey newspapers. Kim is the author of the unpublished middle-grade novel, NED THE MAGE KNIGHT. She is also an artist. Kim lives with her husband on the Jersey Shore.

Marty wouldn't be keeping his treasure. He'd known it last night, hours before meeting Lars for breakfast at the Shore Diner. The only thing changed was how much time he had to get to the marina at Gardner's Basin and his ancient boat.

He stretched a finger toward the huge jar belted into the old Toyota's passenger seat. Only one finger, a light touch on the glass, pulled back before she could react. "Lars says you gotta be worth twenty grand, easy. Maybe he's right. Don't give a damn myself."

He really didn't. Anyway, she wasn't his to sell or not sell. Twenty grand might be nice, but Lars would find a way to get most of Marty's share, like he always did. He wanted Marty to control her—as if anyone could—and keep her close. Lars would never understand how Marty got scared at night, when the air in his trailer turned cold as the sea. Or how her singing swirled around him like smoke, trapping him in the trailer's small living room and pulling him to the jar.

"Don't know why I showed you to him anyway," Marty grumbled. "He says I gotta keep you. Can't do that, though. Can't." Last night he'd made up his mind to release her and since then puzzled why he hadn't done it sooner. When the idea came to him, Marty had felt clean for the first time in days. This morning, though, he'd gotten stupid and showed Lars the mermaid.

Some of the briny liquid sloshed onto the seat from holes

punched in the jar's lid. "You're going home, lady," he said. "I'm taking you back where I found you." He gave a wet cough, took out a cigarette and his lighter. The thing in the jar began turning the lid. Strong she was. Marty lit the cigarette and tossed the lighter on the seat.

"Goody stink," she said through the holes. Her voice had the pitch of a baby's. For the moment, the lid stopped turning. "Yer takes me pier?"

"Nah. My boat. It'll be faster. I'll take you past most of the weekend fishermen."

"Yer boat no good. Drown, yer. Takes me back yer sleep place."

"No," Marty shook his head to clear it. Too much booze, too many cigs. "You, ah, don't belong there, see." Where were the words to explain it? Two days ago he promised to love her forever. Then it was like a bubble broke in his head and he couldn't stand to look at her, in that jar on his card table, like some freak show exhibit. Marty didn't know how he ever had.

"Yer no loves me, Marty?" He didn't answer. "Don't takes me boat, takes me pier, like I tell." There was a drag of sorrow in her voice he felt sure she couldn't feel. She'd told him to lower her to the weedy froth that swirled around the pilings at the end of Caesars' Pier, should she ever displease him.

"Why there?" he'd asked.

"Got family waitin' down pier. Lots of crugs sticks to it. We gots some feast 'round them pilings."

Marty guessed what crugs were. She told him anyway.

"Thems sticking to rocks and piers and bottoms on yer boats. Can't get away. Easy killing thems." Behind the glass, her hideous little face had split into a wide grin, one that showed all her pointed teeth.

The lid started turning again. He heard it scrape loose and swallowed a lump of spit. Her head pressed the underside and the lid tilted up.

"Don't do that," Marty said. "All your water might spill out."

She ignored him. "Yer ain't gonna let that Lars see me no more, is yer? I knows what he wants."

"You do?" Marty laughed, or tried to. "'Course not. Sorry I showed you to him."

Lars was Marty's friend from way back. A petty grifter who got pettier every year. When they'd been young, the two of them would scam old ladies out of their casino winnings. They'd buy the wrinkled darlings a few drinks, do a bit of flirting, then come up with a tear-jerker, hard luck story a few hundred bucks from a kind soul could fix.

Now Marty's curls had gone salt and pepper and he mostly fished from his skiff and collected from Uncle Sam because his bad foot kept him off the big boats. Lars had long ago given up on the comb-over, but he still grifted small time. These days his marks were retiree tourists. Marty sort of liked the one where Lars would lift a slot winner's fat wallet, then pretend to be the good guy who found it dropped and returned it full. He almost always got a decent reward. Way better, he'd told Marty, than getting picked up by the cops with someone else's bread and ID in your back pocket.

Lars was the reason he had to get to Atlantic City and the pier so damn fast. He'd told Marty to take the creature back to the trailer, that he'd show up later with a friend who might have some ideas about what they could do with her.

"Said I'd do that and wait for him," Marty told the mermaid, "but I ain't gonna, and I reckon he's figured that out."

***

Lars stayed two cars back, only speeding up when he saw

Marty pull into Caesars' parking garage. Damn idiot. Did he think he could sneak her past all the tourists and gamblers on the boardwalk? Hell, he probably hadn't even put a towel over the jar. Lars would have. But then Lars wouldn't be stupid enough to let the thing go. Shit, they could make millions.

He'd almost gagged when Marty showed him the little monster. The short man called it a mermaid, but Lars wasn't so sure. It looked more like the dried out fakes you saw in carnival sideshows, the upper half of a monkey sewn onto the lower parts of a fish. But this thing was alive. Its scales had glittered like pirate gold, while its flat-nosed, wide-mouthed monkey face grinned at him from behind the glass.

"Cover that up," he'd said. "Don't let anyone see it." Later, he thought that had been good. They needed the mermaid to be a surprise on the world, not a story some waitress was already telling. At the time though, it was the hideous, toothy face with its I-know-what-you-want smirk.

His "sort of" friend, Nick, who ran a small-time circus around the Jersey Shore every summer, had laughed at him.

"I know what it sounds like, but you gotta see this," Lars had begged.

"You're all kinds of desperate these days, Lars, but I haven't turned stupid," Nick had said before hanging up. He hadn't answered his cell after that. Lars had to get in touch with the right people. But no middlemen. He'd needed to think about who'd pay the most, how to approach them. Maybe that Believe or Not tourist trap near Garden Pier. Yeah, they'd do for a start, then who knew?

***

"I smells it," the mermaid said. She meant the ocean. The creature had allowed Marty to screw the lid down again. Now her slimy lips moved under a punched air hole. She could breathe air or not, as she chose, but very long out of the water, and her gold scales turned green and started to flake away.

Marty too sucked in the ocean scent and found it calmed him. They'd exited the garage, Marty hugging the big jar close to his chest with his left arm, carrying a plastic bucket and coiled fishing line with the other. Sunlight flashed off the glass and made him squint, which was maybe why he didn't see Lars right away.

"Hello, pal. Where you going?" Lars' shadow cut the sun as his big hand fell on Marty's shoulder.

"You know," Marty said. "Fishing."

"Don't be stupid, dude. That fish lady is worth more than you or I ever dreamed of. We'll be rich."

"Don't need money, Lars. Told you that this morning."

"Maybe you don't, but I do." Lars bent to look at the foot-long, fishy freak. Curved like a question mark, with her ugly head turned inward, she looked dead. Her golden scales were turning dull as he watched, but he guessed she wasn't dying. He pushed closer until his glasses clinked, then pulled back and gave Marty a hard look. "I told you to keep that thing covered."

"Sure," Marty said, eyes unfocused. It was Lars who finally threw his worn jacket over the jar.

"Let's you and me head for the boardwalk, eh, Mart?" he said. They started walking, Lars grinning, Marty with gritted teeth. "So," Lars said, as they stepped onto the boardwalk and turned left. "Shall we pay a visit to the museum down the way?"

"No, Lars. I gotta let her go."

"Let's get something straight." Lars stepped in front of Marty. "You and me are partners, pal. We've always been partners.

And partners don't cheat on each other. They don't find gold and hide it." His long index finger poked Marty's chest, just above the jar lid. "I trusted you, Mart, and you went and found yourself something big and didn't even think about letting poor old Lars in on the scam. After I stood by you all these years."

"There's no scam, Lars. And I did show her to you. Just thought you'd like to see something special, before I let her go."

"Give me that." Lars grabbed at the jar.

Marty backed a step, but he'd never been much for muscle. The taller man had always managed him easily. On his second try, Lars jerked her from Marty's grasp. Water banged back and forth inside the jar, but the mermaid, apparently still playing dead, didn't react.

"Your fish lady's gonna earn her keep," Lars said.

For a moment, Marty wondered if Lars had killed her, then he saw her face, with its marble eyes and over-wide jaws, where Lars' jacket had slid aside. She winked at him.

Marty still had the bucket and the fishing line. He waited for Lars to tell him to throw it away, but the other man was staring at the jar. He'd moved his jacket more and Marty could see the gold fish—he sometimes called her that—had her back to them.

"Think it's okay," Lars said.

They started walking again. Lars' long strides kept Marty running. "Wait up," he panted.

There was a hiss from inside the jar. "Marty," she called. "Don't let poor old Lars takes me. Wants yer, Marty. I loves yer."

"No, no, you don't." Marty felt ill.

"I does and me family does, too. Yer likes crugs? I gets yer some, then we goes back to sleep place, yes?"

"What's she talking about?" Lars asked him. "Sounds like gibberish."

Marty shook his head and reached for the jar. "Please, Lars. It's not like you think. Keeping her's no good. Thought I wanted her, see, but it's her wants me."

"Now why would that be, Marty?"

"Don't know." He had puzzled on that as well. Why wouldn't she want to go back to her own kind? She'd offered him crugs before, too, as if she thought he didn't get enough to eat.

"Let me hold her, eh, Lars." Marty put both hands on the jar but couldn't break Lars' grip.

He wondered if the people around them would notice the scuffle, but the crowd broke like water at the front of his boat. Even the lady with the stroller glided deftly away. She glanced at them then looked down at her kid, who wasn't doing anything worse than pounding his stuffed bear against the stroller's front wheel.

Still in full command of the jar, Lars surprised Marty with small talk. "Why'd you take her home in the first place, Mart?" he asked. "She really save your life, like you said in the diner?"

Marty nodded as he looked up. Lars' fat head acted like a sun umbrella so he didn't need to shade his eyes. "Just wanted to get a better look at her, you know." He'd used his empty bait bucket, filling it quickly from the bit of ocean sloshing around in the bottom of his boat. Still coughing up salt water, he'd grabbed her finny hand, dropped her into the bucket, slammed on the lid, then set his tackle box on top. It only worked because she'd been exhausted herself, from pulling him back into the boat. "I was always gonna bring her back," he lied.

"Then you got a good look and saw dollar signs. But you

don't have the brains for this, pal. Why didn't you come see old Lars right away?"

Marty eyed the mermaid's jar. They were approaching Caesars' shopping pier. If he grabbed it now and ran for the doors, he could maybe get through to the end of the pier. Close to where she wanted. But no, it wouldn't work. He was too weak and too scared Lars or someone else would stop him. Wish it was my boat was under that pier, he thought, instead of the lifeguard's.

Then Marty surprised himself and Lars. He grabbed the jar, pulled it away, and ran. He passed the doors to the mall and kept going. Marty didn't run so good these days, though, what with his bad foot. He slowed to a half-run, and Lars almost caught up.

A security guard started toward them, definitely looking at the jar. Marty looked, too. Lars' jacket had slipped down, and the mermaid was perfectly visible.

"Hey, old guys," the guard called. "Keep it to a walk, okay?" Then he turned away, shaking his head.

They both slowed, Marty wondering if the guard saw mermaids every day, so his was no surprise.

"What gives?" Lars' panted up behind him.

"He seen her, Lars. Didn't even care." Marty dropped the plastic bucket so he could get a better grip on the jar. "Maybe you won't make no money, see." He kept walking, banged into a young guy, got called an asshole.

"God-damned kids, these days," Lars said, still sucking for breath. "Hold up, Mart." He bent over his beer belly, hands on his knees. Marty didn't know what else to do, so he stopped and waited for Lars to straighten up.

The mermaid's hands were tucked inward. When she did that, the webbed skin running from her lower ribs to her wrist, like narrow bats' wings, made it look as if she had fins. Then she untucked her hands. Squirrel hands, Marty thought. She turned one palm up and bent the clawed index finger, beckoning him. Marty put his ear to the lid.

"Takes me to yer trailer, Marty," she said in her babyish voice. "If Lars no lets yer, kill him."

"What?" Marty's tongue felt thick.

"Lets me out. I bites him. Makes blood. Goody licking."

"N-no."

"Now, what's she saying?" Lars stood straight.

"Nothing. She's just, ah, just wants to go home."

"Don't think so." He let Lars imagine she meant home to the sea. "Give me the jar, Mart."

Marty looked down at the lid. One of her eyes was visible through an air hole. Why not, he thought. Why not let Lars have the thing? Marty had wanted to keep her, to hear her songs so badly, he'd cried whenever he felt guilty about a sentient being living in a jar. Now he couldn't wait to be rid of her, something she seemed not to have guessed.

Then he looked at his friend. Lars' bald dome gleamed in the sunlight, his fringe was going grey. The thick, black-rimmed glasses made his eyes huge and time had carved deep crevasses around his mouth. He was tall, had been handsome once. Marty had envied Lars, looked up to him, admired and tried to emulate him. Lars had been the leader, the guy with ideas, also the guy who saw to it they always made out—somehow.

Marty glanced down at the mermaid again and knew what he would do. He spun away and made for the beach ramp, running again. His feet hit sand, sloughed through it. Marty's foot hurt bad, but he didn't care. He angled away toward the pier, moving faster than he had in years.

Lars was after him, of course, closing fast with his longer legs. Marty reached the lifeboat, parked sideways to the surf,

19

tossed the jar in the bottom and pushed at the boat's stern. It moved, but not much. He tried swinging it around to get the bow in the water. Lousy way to launch a boat, he thought. How'd they ever get it floating in time to save a swimmer?

As the bow rose on a wave, Lars slammed into him, shoving Marty and the boat deep into the surf. The little man leapt over the gunwale, turned and grabbed the oars.

"Come back here," Lars yelled. "Damn it, Marty, don't be stupid." He waded in. Marty tried but wasn't fast enough. Lars had hold of the side of the boat.

Marty glanced at the jar. It was tipped at an angle against the middle bench and the lid was turning—fast. Lars reached for it.

"Don't," Marty shouted. He was too late. The lid clanked into the bottom of the boat and she exploded through the opening. The mermaid was stunning, the way she landed on Lars' arm, slithered up it, clamped her jaws over his face.

The really horrible thing was Lars didn't scream. He couldn't, Marty guessed, with teeth like curved daggers stitching his mouth closed. Marty could see his bulged eyes and the blood, splashing everywhere. Lars pulled at the monster, but she was slick with sea water, slime, and his blood. He couldn't get a grip. He backed to the sand, fell on his rear, then went down onto his back.

"Lars!" Marty could finally move. He couldn't turn the boat so he jumped out, stumbled through the waves and fell on his knees. She let go then, twisting herself around to look at Marty.

The little man opened his mouth to call for help and made a soft squeak. Didn't matter anyway; Lars was dead. Where his face had been was a red pit. One eye remained, sort of, and the bottom of his chin. Blood turned his Hawaiian shirt black, sank into the sand around his head, pinked the foam that slipped in and out around his big feet.

She slid off Lars, came to Marty. "Goody fun," she said. "Takes me yer trailer Marty. I wants to sing to yer." Marty got to his feet, shaking like a malaria victim. He walked toward the boat, which had washed back onto the beach, threw up in it, then retrieved her jar and filled it with seawater.

She wriggled inside and let him screw the lid down. Marty stood, holding the heavy glass against his chest. He didn't see the lifeguard and guessed he wouldn't. People were sitting on the beach not twenty feet away, yet no heads turned, no fingers pointed. He felt bad leaving Lars, but was there a choice?

Marty headed for the parking lot where he'd get into his car, he and the mermaid. He'd drive home to his trailer and set her down on the card table. No one would stop him; the cops wouldn't find them. And when it got dark outside, she would sing.

MINOTAUR

R.S. BOHN

R.S. Bohn lives in a suburb outside of Detroit. She enjoys craft beer, Skor bars, and growing lavender. A Pushcart Prize nominee eons ago, she now writes short stories while also working on her first novel.

Noani's period had gone on for four weeks, bleeding through supplies, and the metal bin where they were kept was nearly empty. The expedition had no medical personnel. There was a small village eight hours' drive, but she refused to think of leaving, both afraid of what the men would think and afraid they would find something without her. She was not afraid of what the bleeding meant; her mother and aunt had both died of tumors in the uterus. If cancer were to strike here, on the taiga, then so be it. She thought, but did not write it in her journal, that if she were to die, she hoped they would find the return to civilization with her body too taxing; after all, there was barely enough room in the vehicles as it was, with equipment crammed into every available bit of space. The peaty earth was already dug in six places. They could lower her in—roll her in for all she cared—and cover her with mounds of damp, brown soil. Perhaps another expedition would find her in a thousand years; perhaps she would be looked upon with wonder by them, touched by hands a dozen generations younger than her, a step forward in time and collapsed on itself all at once.

Swallowing another three pills—she was constant, at the limits of prescribed amounts, keeping the pain to a dull writhing within her abdomen—she walked out of the tent, the wind catching her up and swallowing her as if she was the pill, the thing it must take.

"Together!" shouted a tall blonde man, and he and two others swept a snapping blue tarp up over their newest hole in the ground.

"Why are you covering it?" she shouted over the wind.

He pointed at the darkening sky, where clouds rolled in over the distant mountains, and got to work with the mallet, pounding in stakes to keep the tarp down. Judging by the wind, the tarp would be tattered by evening. She didn't relish the thought of another day lost due to weather; rain, not uncommon in early fall on the steppes, had battered their timeline without mercy. They were already behind six days. Still, she wasn't due back at the university until November, a four-week intensive she was assigned to teach awaiting her. Greek myth and modern Turkey. They would expect Amazons; she'd give them volcanoes and arks, instead.

"Stop," she said. Leer glanced up. "It won't rain for a couple of hours. I'll dig."

"It'll rain any minute," he said, continuing to pound a stake.

"No, it won't. Stop and I'll work. I'll finish the tarp myself." She reached down to take the mallet, but he pulled it back.

"Go back to your tent."

She knelt down. "Go back to yours. This is my operation."

"Our site, Noani." He stopped, sighing. "Fine. Go down, dig. But if it starts to rain and you're not up, I'll drag you out of there if I have to."

Her smile was thin. "I'm sure you will, Max."

She climbed beneath at the incline side, the end of the tarp slapping at her as she entered. She heard Max telling the others they were done for the day, that she would work for a bit and then join them. A lie, which they would know. How often did she join them? Meals, sometimes not even those. Their shoulders occasionally touched hers while they worked, a knee in her line of vision, but they moved around each other like ghosts, the men talking, joking. As if she was the ghost.

The odd blue light beneath the tarp and bits of gray sunlight peeping under the edges was not enough. She turned on an LED lantern and unrolled her tools. Taking a trowel, she began to chip away at a bit of gray, clay-like earth, the object beneath beginning finally to show itself. Today, she thought, would be the day she would reveal it for what it was, rain be damned.

Her stomach twisted, and between her legs, another sickening gush of liquid. She paused for breath. Another tap with the trowel, and a chunk of earth fell away.

A horn. She'd expected it, having seen a bit of the curving white shape. An hour passed. It grew larger, longer, as still she scraped. The rain pattered lightly, brief bursts that meant nothing.

Another hour, and the second horn was nearly free. She chewed the inside of her lip, thinking.

An aurochs this far north would be a find; she'd come for something else, something more prehistoric, but an aurochs bull would satisfy.

Another light tap-tap-tapping, and the horn, half an arm's length from its twin, stood out. She turned her attention lower, and began to uncover the animal's skull. The wind cracked the tarp above her.

Tufts of hair, dark and bristly, were exposed where white bone should have been. She paused. Got her brush.

An aurochs hide, preserved. She could not breathe.

Above, the wind settled as she touched the tip of her brush to the bony precipice, before it took up again in a long, shivering low. It reminded her of the cattle she'd seen once in the Scottish Highlands, red and shaggy and scattered across rocks and crags beneath a steely sky. The Scottish cattle were shorter than aurochs, more compact. The aurochs resembled an African type of cattle, more Watusi than oxen.

She had noted cows since childhood; the luminous, doe-eyed Jersey cows that inhabited a farm by her big island home had been her favorite. Trips to Somalia and Kenya had given her an appreciation for the velvety, wrinkled hides of local cattle there. She sometimes thought that if she were to give up archaeology, give up all this digging in places too hot or too cold, she might take up farming. A garden of no less than an acre, and chickens, one or two cows. Which was ridiculous, considering that she would probably die with a trowel in her hand, in some pit. Possibly this one.

This pit was ten by fifteen feet, and currently ten feet deep. It hugged the tree line, which is where they camped, giving them some defense from the rain. The heavy, dark trunks of the pines were always damp, moss riding their bark to the first or second set of branches. She and the men hung their laundry between the trees; their kitchen was strung high, even scrubbed pots, so as not to attract bears. Their garbage was taken far enough from camp to be disposed of without issue. They had started this dig the previous spring, and the entire area seemed homey to her, now that she had learned its bushes and trees and rocks.

So many rocks. The men piled them by their tents, some-times, and sometimes left them scattered across the ground, like shattered bones.

The soil fell away with ease, clumps thumping to the floor. A dark brown cheek was exposed, heavily muscled. She touched it with a gloved finger, gingerly. How had this come to be? An aurochs this far north, and so well preserved in strange clay earth not often seen in the taiga? Was it alone? It had to be at least four hundred years old, if not much older. But it looked as if it had been buried twenty years ago.

Noani chiseled, flakes of clay falling more rapidly, revealing the closed eye, the set mouth, and finally, the impossible roundness of a nose, nostrils filled with clay. She shivered in the cold.

The wind scraped at the tarp overhead. The first real bullets of rain hit, and she picked up a small brush. Swirled it around in a nostril, clearing it. Did the same for the other. Small hairs stuck up from the nose, spiky and dark. Removing her glove, she held a hand to it, afraid to touch, but wanting to.

Warmth ghosted across her palm.

Noani jerked back.

"Hey! Rain's here! Time to come up!" Max lifted the tarp and peered underneath. "Noani? Come up."

She turned. "I'll be right up."

"No. Now, Noani. Look, it's really coming down."

It was. The light patter had become a hard *rat-a-tat-tat*, and already, she could see trickles of water along the edges of the pit.

"What's that? You got quite a bit more," said Max.

She grabbed an oilcloth and draped it over the horns. Clicked off the lantern. Max climbed down.

"I'll help you get your tools," he said.

"I've got it," she said, gathering everything in a rush. "Let's go."

She waited for him to go first, impatiently motioning with a jerk of her head. He climbed back up, and they trotted for the tents.

"What pit are you in tomorrow?" she called through the rain.

"What?"

"What pit?" she shouted. "Tomorrow?"

"Oh," he said. "That one, I suppose."

"No," she said. "You and Travis take pit two."

He frowned. "We'll talk tomorrow."

"Pit two," she said, standing outside her tent, tools in her arms. The rain was a downpour, both of them soaked. Max's blond hair had become dark, plastered to his face.

"Fine. Whatever. We'll discuss it tomorrow, Noani," he called over the rain.

"Two," she shouted. "You and Travis. Pit two."

He shook his head and ran off for his own tent, and she hurried into hers, dripping water onto the floor. She dropped the tools and began to undress, stripping down quickly. Toweling off her damp skin, she looked in her metal supplies box and took out a pad, thick as a novel.

Noani rehydrated soup over the little burner in her tent, not bothering to join the men. Let them think it was just the rain, keeping her inside.

And if she did not bleed to death, she would uncover the rest of the aurochs after the rain stopped. By herself.

She slept, the rain pounding on her tent like a thousand hooves, and dreamed of lovers from long ago, their breath warm on her cheek.

***

Noani did not remember her aunt. There was a picture of her, her mother's sister, faded sepia and framed in tarnished gold, on the wall above the couch. Right beside it was a picture of her great-grandmother, who had spoken only Hawaiian and died just after her seventh child had succumbed to typhoid at age two. There were other pictures, in black and white, or sepia, or faded color squares, all along the wall. Noani knelt backwards on the couch when she was a girl, elbows on the puffy top of it, looking at the parade of portraits and saying their names: Fritzi, Aluala, Callie, Molly Keanna. There were men, too, who died of eating too much, smoking too much, but it was the women who died of nothing much at all: cancer, little black beads strung through their abdomens like leis.

She liked Fritzi's picture best: the stiff pin curls, the dark lipstick, the eyes like two half-smiles. Noani had tried curling her hair many times as a teenager; she'd been left with ringlets and frizz.

Fritzi was outspoken, they said. She'd had many suitors, drawn by her laugh. Went to all the dances. Wore a bikini to a cliff jumping, and was the only girl there who'd jump. Her top had come off, torn by the force of her entry into the swirling water. Another boy had given her his shirt to cover her; they said she'd wrapped it around her torso like a bandage and refused to give it back.

There were a hundred gods on the islands, but for Noani there was only one: Fritzi, her patron saint.

All the other gods had long been unearthed.

She thought of Fritzi as she descended into the pit the next morning. They'd never had much in common, Fritzi and Noani. Fritzi had been the third daughter. Noani the only one. This was pit four, and perhaps their designated rankings had come together in this.

She paused, blinking. Perhaps she'd lost too much blood. Deities didn't exist, no more than ghosts were real. There was no portent in the order of birth, and the only thing that would link the long-dead aunt and her wayfaring niece would be an early death, childless.

Moribund didn't suit her, she thought, frowning. She was serious, even grim, but not morose.

The lantern on, she slid the oilcloth from the aurochs horns.

It was an amazing head, enormous and heavy, not elegantly

sloped like a Jersey. There was power in its breadth. She longed to touch it with her bare fingers, to feel the cheek and stroke beneath the jaw.

And it was an amazing find. She was convinced it was an aurochs now, and not some overly large bull that had wandered from its domesticated herd and died out here on the taiga. The angle of the horns, how they curved out and then front, as if they could scoop a man and toss him. The sheer size of it! Yes, this was a creature only a big cat could take down, if that.

She set to revealing the neck, further intrigued by how the flesh did not peel away easily, did not shrivel and turn to husk.

Of course. Because the animal was not old. This was no aurochs. It was some modern cattle, dark and huge, to be sure, but not the near-mythical aurochs.

The trowel shook in her hand. Noani closed her eyes, pressing back tears. She had come out here, hoping to find pottery and tools of prehistoric hunter-gatherers, the mark of culture's hard march north, and instead had found some modern-day farmer's lost bull.

What would the men think, that she'd told them to stay away so that she could unearth a cow? Travis and Callahan avoided her; graduate students, she'd had to cajole and coerce them when they should've leapt at the chance to come along. But they'd studied under her, and she was sure they found her prickly, stubborn and unfriendly. And Max, the only one who would come with her when she called without her having to persuade him, the only one who seemed to believe that Noani could find something that no one else had—perhaps this time would be the last. She'd be back to begging for funds, groveling for partners.

She would never be free of the demands of the university,

when teaching brought in the only real money. Her expeditions were not fruitful. Her dream of living site-to-site, always a pit outside her tent, would not be realized when backers couldn't rationalize it.

Sniffing, she opened her eyes. She'd dig out the bull.

Black eyes, liquid and deep, looked back at her.

Up above, she heard the men walking around, talking and joking. They were walking to pit two.

Those eyes stared, unblinking, a trace of dampness around their rims.

Perhaps she was wrong, and they'd been open all along.

No. They would be hollows, then. Eyes rotted fast. There should be nothing in the socket, nothing at all.

The springy ground muffled his steps. She heard him call a moment before he pulled the edge of the tarp back.

"Sun's out. I'll take this off for you," he said. "How's it coming?"

"Leave it," she said. "It rains so often, I'll probably need it in an hour." She attempted a small laugh. Max frowned and leaned his head in.

"Noani. What is it? Those are some horns," he said.

"Yes," she said, nodding at the thing behind her and moving her body a bit to block it. "Looks like somebody's bull got lost or buried somehow, and we found it. So. Not anything, really, but I thought I'd dig it out a bit more, see if I can find anything interesting."

"In a lost cow?" Max frowned. "Seems frivolous, if you don't mind me saying. We've got what appears to be a stone circle in two. Maybe a campfire. Why don't you come over and see what you think?"

"I will," she said. "I just want to dig this out a little more, that's all. I know, it sounds strange, but there's something about it I think is interesting."

"All right. If you don't come over to two, I'll get you at lunch. Okay?"

"Fine. Thanks, Max."

"Noani, are you all right?"

Max, always watching her a bit too closely. She clenched her jaw, wanting to tell him to mind his own business, but instead said, "I'm fine. Tired, I guess. The weather."

He nodded. "It's wearing on us all. If we come back, let's push it to summer next time, eh?"

"Sure," she said, but she knew that she wouldn't come back. She would unearth this bull and that would be that. Whatever she found or did not find, she would not be back to this site.

Max got up from his crouch and left, and Noani turned back to the bull. Its eyes were closed, tightly shut, and the dampness had worsened to a trickle, cutting a wet path down both cheeks.

***

The men passed around cold leftover stew—mostly carrots and onions—slathered on hard bread, the juices from the stew vaguely making the bread chewy. She did her best to look at them, to smile at the words they were saying, though she knew the smiles were ill timed, her glances making them uneasy.

Passing for normal was difficult under mundane circumstances; it was not Fritzi's charisma she summoned, but her independence, her strength. Her bravery. She'd thought those far more valuable qualities, but at the moment, she wished she could relax, charm them with a grin. Make them forget about pit four.

They talked about how odd it was to find cattle out here, but some nomadic families kept cows for milk. Goats were more common. She agreed, and said she knew it was trivial, but she wondered what had happened to this one.

That was the truth. She did wonder. The bull's neck did not extend back from its head, as expected, but straight down. Who would bury a bull standing straight up? She wondered if the neck would soon stop—a ragged cut, indicating where the head had been severed before being dropped into a hole and buried. Some sort of religious omen, a pagan offering.

Yes, she told herself. It would end at the neck.

Max held out his hands, demonstrating the width of the horns. Travis and Callahan were impressed. Wanted to see.

"No," she said. They stopped at her abrupt intrusion. "I mean, no. I want it to be a surprise, when I get the whole thing exposed."

The men exchanged confused looks.

"Well," said Max. "The radio, near as I can make out, says more rain in a couple of days. Why don't we drive back to town and wait it out? I think we all need a break."

Noani nodded along with the others, though with less enthusiasm.

She wouldn't go into town. Didn't like the staring, as if she was an outsider, a stranger—which she was. But it made her feel as if she couldn't breathe, suffocated her anytime she was around people she didn't know, people who expected her to try to make conversation, even if they spoke another language.

But she could rely on her foreignness, conversely, to keep strangers at bay. It was worse, sometimes, being around people she should, at least nominally, know.

"Good," said Max. "We'll pack up tomorrow." He paused.

"Noani?"

She sucked in a breath. Stood, though she was dizzy.

The men were silent.

"Noani," said Max in a low voice, setting his plate aside and standing. He took her elbow.

She looked down, where they all stared for a moment, wide-eyed, and looked away, embarrassed. Her canvas pants were soaked with blood between her legs.

***

She snapped at Max, who tried to help her to her tent. Stopped short of shrieking when he came to check on her fifteen minutes later. Jesus, she snarled. It was only a menstrual cycle.

She thought he'd leave, uncomfortable with it, but when she came out, newly supplied and in fresh pants, he was waiting nearby. He looked up.

"Don't ask if I'm all right," she said, staring at him.

He raised an eyebrow, cocked his head. "Okay, I won't." He produced a small, leather-bound flask and wiggled it in the air.

"Booze, Max?"

"Only schnapps. My mom always said it helped."

"Schnapps for cramps?"

"And for burnt dinners, parent-teacher meetings, and putting clothes on the line." He shrugged. "Kind of a cure-all, in our house."

"You had some kind of childhood."

"You could say that." He held it out. She surprised herself and took it, unscrewing the cap and sniffing. "Blackberry," he said.

She sipped. "I prefer cinnamon."

"It'll be on the manifest, next expedition." He smiled. "Sorry you're feeling shitty. So, do you want help on pit four?"

She took a breath and said nothing.

"You probably don't want help in four. But I'm asking." He took the schnapps and swallowed, wiping his mouth after with his wrist. "Look, Noani, this is our second time at the site. We haven't come up with much. The board will withdraw funding for another trip."

"So... you want me to forget about the bull, and help in two?"

He shook his head and grinned. "No. I want you to dig out the damn bull, and if you want help, I'll do it. Just do it by tomorrow, and if you can't, oh well. We're going to town, and we're going to eat real, hot food. Even if it is sausages and cabbages. And we're going to drink beer. You included. Well, you can pass on the beer if you want. But we're getting out of here for a day or two. We need it. It's... the trees, or something. Like they're closing in."

They looked at the forest behind their camp, the spruces bent and snaking unevenly upwards. The soft ground routinely froze and sank, twisting the trunks.

The air smelled like pine needles and wet earth.

"Out here?" She laughed softly, gesturing to the space on the other side, the yellow-brown rolling hillocks of the taiga.

"Mm. Do you want our help?"

She shook her head.

"My help?"

She shook her head again. "Thanks, Max. But I want to do this by myself."

He didn't understand, she could see that. It didn't matter, however; she took a swig of schnapps and—in a strange moment that left her off-kilter—winked at Max before heading back to the pit.

Her stomach felt much better.

***

Fritzi, she decided. That's where the wink had come from. It was so unlike Noani. Had she ever winked at anyone?

Another clod of clay fell. It was odd, this clay. Almost foreign. It reminded her of a dig in eastern Macedonia once; they'd been on the border of Greece, and the clay was thick, gray-brown, and dried out the hands until they bled.

She was used to that, bleeding. Tools slipped. Rocks protruded where one hadn't noticed them before. Hands cracked from being in dirt all the damn day.

She was not used to thinking about Max. She found herself idly wondering if he would've been taken by her Aunt Fritzi, if he'd have been one of the many men who called, who asked her out. She'd liked blondes, they said. Told everyone she was getting off the island and going to California, going to meet herself a tall blonde man in a suit and hat.

Fritzi loved the sun, loved people. Noani loved the shadows of the pits, especially with tarps overhead, or climbing into caves and catacombs where the sun was only a memory.

The sun on the taiga was weak, but still she'd blocked it out with the tarp. The autumn rains were frequent, true, but she liked it in the darkness, with only the LED lanterns.

More clay. She'd been worried the head wouldn't be able to support itself, but it held up just fine, despite her carving out the area beneath it. She'd gone around the neck, discovering what could only be, like sunlight in caves, a memory of muscles. But what muscles they'd been! Immensely thick, rippling dark waves that extended the length of the neck.

She imagined the shoulder would be next. Or not. Perhaps it would, finally, end.

She peered up. The rain had started again. Hadn't Max said it would be a couple of days?

Holding up her trowel, she listened. The rain quickened, the winds picking up, snapping at the edge of the tarp. At this rate, it would be in tatters soon.

She sighed. Max would come get her if it looked like a storm. She scraped away at the clay, waiting for the inevitable. And there it was: her name, the tarp edge being lifted.

"I'm coming right now," she called, and placed the trowel back in the tool roll. She reached for the lantern, clicking it off.

The darkness shifted. She took a step, hesitant. Something moved, rumbled beneath her feet and around her. She took another step, eyes searching the gloom. Was it an earthquake? The pit collapsing? Her insides jittered; her vision unfocused.

"Noani!"

She buckled, falling to the ground. Her guts felt as if they would dislodge themselves in a moment. She put a hand on the earth to feel its trembling.

Max grasped her beneath the armpits and hauled her up. He was saying her name, but it was so far off. She told him to get out of the cave, that it was going to collapse, and it was all right. She'd stay.

Shouting. Travis and Callahan, clambering down into pit four and taking her by her assorted limbs. She wanted desperately to tell them to stop, they were pulling her apart.

The climb to the surface hurt; her head ached from the light.

She cried, trying to reach back for the bull. His eyes were open again, she could feel it.

They were open, and they were looking right at her.

***

Her mouth was dry. She mumbled for water. Immediately, a glass was presented at her lips. She sipped.

The rain hadn't stopped. Max pressed the back of his hand against her forehead, his skin cool.

"Noani, can you hear me?"

"Course," she said, voice hoarse. "You're right next to me."

He smiled and took the glass away. They were in her tent, she realized.

She licked her lips and looked around, then up at Max, hovering beside her. His face was drawn, pale mustache stretched over his lips.

"What happened?"

"I don't know, but as soon as the rain lets up, we're taking you to town. Maybe farther, if their doctor doesn't know what's wrong."

She sighed. "It's nothing."

"Noani, I'm no expert, but something is wrong."

She struggled to sit up, but fell back. She felt weak. Tired.

"I just need some sleep."

"Then get some. I'll wake you when it's time to go."

"I'm not going anywhere, Max."

He smiled. "Not this time, Noani. This time, you do as I say."

She attempted to stare back, the patented Noani death glare, but it dissolved immediately, with no will behind it. Looking down, she realized he was holding her hand.

"I just want to sleep a bit more," she said.

He nodded, and as she closed her eyes, she saw him watching her, the corners of his warm, brown eyes creased with concern.

She drifted off, thinking of the pit.

***

It was still raining when she woke, and dark. There was a lantern giving a low bluish-white glow at the table nearby, and a blanket that was hers but had not been on the chair. Max had left, she supposed. Gone for food, a break.

She sat up, swaying a bit, and pushed off the covers. She was not soaked in blood, which was unexpected. Her thighs were bare, caramel skin prickling with goose bumps.

Clean pants were nearby. She didn't pause to think about Max undressing her; she pulled on pants, grabbed a waterproof jacket, and pulling the hood over her head, she opened the tent flap.

She hadn't checked the time. It didn't matter.

All that mattered was finishing the excavation.

Taking the lantern, she hurried across muddy ground. There was light in one of the other tents; the men were up. Max would come to check on her soon. When he discovered her missing, he would surely check pit four. She would show him she felt fine, and that the rain meant nothing. Tell him to go back, leave her alone.

She slipped on the ground at the pit's edge and fell, bumping, to her butt. She hissed.

A sore back. Just another small inconvenience.

Getting to her feet was difficult. She put a hand to the pit wall to steady her. It was damp, and her fingers sunk in a little.

A few steps, her breathing hard, and she lifted the lantern.

Someone had been digging in her pit. Clumps of clay were piled on the floor of the pit, not even shoveled to one side. Her heart thumped in anger. She took another step, holding out the lantern.

Its eyes were open. She stared into them, into the liquid black that seemed to be seeing her, and let her gaze drift downward.

The neck ended. There was no ragged slash. Flesh, darkened with dirt, seamlessly ran into the furred neck of the bull.

She reached out, a trembling fingertip touching the place where a human collarbone, impossibly, sat.

Its skin trembled in response. Her eyes snapped up.

It let out a breath, hot and strong, and snuffled. Strained— she could feel it, see the muscles tighten and tense.

It wanted to break free. It wanted loose of the clay, so heavy and dense, that held it down. Its mouth opened, sucking in air, and she imagined in horror the weight of all that clay upon its chest, its head, the impossibility of taking a breath—

The impossibility of such a thing *existing*. Her head swirled with imagery, all of it from books.

A lost bull. Yes. Lost to time and myth. She was standing in a pit on the taiga, and she had found something that ought never to have existed.

She had found something.

It groaned, straining against the wall of clay that held it back. Noani scrabbled for tools, a pick, a trowel, and held them to the body in front of her. It paused its exertions to stare at her. She should be careful, she could damage it.

It allowed the trowel's edge to scrape, carefully, at skin. But it didn't tremble, didn't shake. Nor did her hands. Faster, and faster, she scuffed and scraped. Clay fell on her boots.

It jerked, and a shoulder was free. Another jerk, and clay cracked, but held.

"Easy," she told it. "Easy."

She wouldn't have much time. Max would come for her soon. He wouldn't understand. Noani didn't know if she understood, even when the truth was right there, where she could touch it.

Thunder like crumpled wood, like breaking trees, echoed over them. She caught the creature's gaze, and saw a wagon, drawn by nervous, foam-flecked horses, rumbling over uneven ground. Wheels sunk into soft earth. The sun hid behind gray clouds, and inside the wagon, inside the massive wooden box, its cargo shivered and moaned and bled and tried to take a breath, but all was cold clay.

She tore her eyes away, and dragged a hand down the exposed chest. Bits of clay rolled under her fingers. The clay earth of its home, packed with rocks along tunnels it roamed endlessly, the only light a few torches, forever burning out.

A deep breath, the deepest one of all, and it bellowed. Noani fell back, and the walls of the pit started to crumble.

It would not wait. Could not. Not another minute, another second. Roaring, its mouth a yawning cavern with long, stiff tongue, it heaved itself into the pit.

The clay sucked at it, unwilling to release its captive, but with a final shake, the Minotaur stumbled forward.

Her heart beat, almost painful in her chest, and her vision clouded, but she stood straight. A step... another... The last steps in a long journey, she realized. She had traveled all over, to find so many dead ends, but this was what she had been searching for all along.

Her arm outstretched, she walked over chunks of earth, fingertips stretching. Reaching for it. It held its enormous head high, looking down at her as its chest expanded, taking in breath after breath.

She touched that broad plain, pressed her palm flat against flesh flushed with warmth.

The Minotaur shoved, and Noani backed up, falling over clods of clay and hitting the wall of the pit. Getting to her feet, back to the wall, she waited. It lowered its head.

Huge horns imbedded in the earth to either side of her head. Its nose was inches from her. Its breath stank, she realized, like blood. A scent she knew well. The iron scent of blood.

There was no more fear. She would dive from this cliff. And if the water pulled her under...

In those eyes she saw longing, and hate, and sorrow. She saw young men and women held limp in the Minotaur's hands. She saw a man who came to the Minotaur with no fear, but a sword. A hero who glowed like a hundred torches in the maze, who placed his palm upon the monster's chest just as Noani had, and whose touch made promises.

A fierce protectiveness rose up inside her. *I'll never betray you.*

Her hands grasped a horn on either side. She saw herself in those black eyes: dark braid hanging over one shoulder, the sheen of sweat on her round face, and her own eyes, as black and determined as his.

Max tore back the tarp and shouted her name. For an instant, he was stunned, frozen. Then he jumped into the pit, sliding on the wet ground near the entrance, and the Minotaur jerked its horns free of the wall and turned to face him.

"No!" Noani didn't know who she screamed at, or what it meant—it was simply *No*, no one else, not here, no, no, *no*.

The Minotaur barreled towards him, and Max held out his arms.

God, not Max. Not Max, oh please.

If the Minotaur heard, she did not know, only that it turned its head and swept Max aside with those massive horns at that last moment, the man slamming into a wall and crumpling to the ground.

It climbed the slope in two strides, slashing the tarp as it rose into the air above the pit. Noani clambered after it, slipping on the slope and falling to her knees.

Her guts wrenched themselves in two. She clawed at her stomach, pain spearing her from front to back. Gritting her teeth, she hauled herself up the remaining feet, fingers digging into the mud at the pit's edge.

It was dark, no moonlight in the storm, and the rain stung her face in vicious, needling hits. She could not see him.

Behind her, somewhere in the pit, Max groaned. She hesitated. Part of her wanted to go after the creature. Part of her wanted to go to Max. And part of her wanted to rip itself free of her body, an alien parasite straight out of the movies.

She sat on her bottom and slid carefully down into the pit. Max was sitting up, holding one shoulder. She walked slowly over and sat next to him.

"Broken?"

He eyed her. "It takes more than a farmer's lost bull to break me, Noani." He winced. "But the shoulder, no. Probably just dislocated."

"I can do that. Put your shoulder back in."

"You like causing me pain, don't you?"

She leaned her head against his good shoulder. "Oh, Max."

His cheek was warm atop her head. "Oh, Noani," he whispered. "What have you done?"

The tarp crinkled, and Travis and Callahan peered down in the light of their lanterns.

"Find her? What happened?"

Noani was silent.

"Fell on the damn slope in the damn mud. Help me out," said Max.

The two men, wary of Noani, as if coming too close or looking at her too long might cause a disaster, helped Max to his
feet with no more than a cursory, "Are you all right?" to her.

They were concerned, she could see. And at their wit's end
with her.

Maybe, she thought, she was at her wit's end with herself.

There was no argument when they decided to leave at first
light to find a hospital—for both of them. Noani, exhausted
and weak, looked for prints in the ground before they left,
but there was nothing special about any of the indentations.
They all looked like the footprints of men, and if some lacked
the tread of boots, well, those were hardly remarkable otherwise.

Max sat in the backseat of the SUV beside her, giving her
thoughtful looks but saying nothing. And when the vehicle
jolted over yet another hillock, and his hand slid atop hers,
she didn't pull it away. He closed his fingers over hers and
squeezed.

It was a damn shame, she thought, that just when she'd
found her bravery, she should have to die.

She squeezed back, and mercifully fell into sleep, and in her
dreams, she stood at the center of a labyrinth, with white
stones spiraling all around her feet.

***

There was a moment when Max knew: standing on the lanai
of her mother's house, Noani wore a red dress, wrapped
around her and tucked, and a thread along the hem had
come free. It was just above her knee. He saw that red thread
and wanted to pull on it, unravel the entire thing until it was
piled at her feet.

He had come to see her, all the way from Connecticut.
Maybe he should've known then. At least on the plane, all

those hours in a seat that gave him a terrible crick in his neck.

He'd known better than to ask how she was doing, and at any rate, she looked wonderful. Her emails had been forthcoming and, progressively, warmer. Benign tumors. She'd opted for a hysterectomy. Such strange things to tell a man she'd known for years but who knew little beyond the lines on her face that meant she was angry, or afraid, or—

New lines. He read them then, as spring winds fed them scents of plumeria and ginger. Lines of determination. Those he'd seen before. And...

"Of course," he said. "Of course I'll go."

"Just you and me," she said.

He paused. Their emails had been honest, even teasing sometimes, but of all the things they'd talked about, this one thing had been left unsaid. Well, perhaps two things.

"And if we find it?" he said, voice low. "Do you intend to feed me to it, as a sacrifice?"

She beamed up at him. "No. You're much too skinny. Wouldn't feed an iguana." She became serious. "There was a sighting in Siberia."

He nodded. "I saw it online. They're calling it the horned Yeti. No pictures, though."

"Doesn't matter. Has to be him." She put her hands on the railing and stared into the forest. "The university is letting me come back in September. I can leave now."

"I've got another week, Noani. That's it. Not enough time. We'd have a few days, at best."

"Good enough."

He thought about it, the particulars, the planning involved. "Then there's flights—"

"There's one tomorrow afternoon, back to the mainland. I've

got it all scheduled from there." She put her hand on his. "Please, Max."

"Fine," he said. "Fine. Let's go. Find your lost bull." He gazed around at the lush, green forest, at the lanai with its two chairs, where he could plausibly sit forever. "What do we do until then?"

She grinned. "Ever been cliff diving?"

INDULGENCE
TAMMY SALYER

Tammy is an independently published speculative fiction writer and freelance editor. Her fangirl goal in life is to sing karaoke with Commander Mark Hadfield and novelist Neil Gaiman aboard the International Space Station. But she'd settle for digestifs and tea with them somewhere on Earth, too. She'd love to hear from you! Stop by and say hi at her website (www.tammysalyer. com) or join her newsletter tribe for novel and story news (http://eepurl.com/XfuJD).

It's the first genuine smile Marla has had since the world ended.

Well, ended is putting it a bit dramatically. But changed, definitely changed. No more cheeseburgers, no more greasy fries, no more clove cigarettes or rye martinis. She misses the martinis the most: the glistening ice chips dripping languidly down the inverted triangle of her cocktail glass, gin swirling around the olive like an orbiting cloud of divinity. And the clove cigarettes that made everything smell like a Manhattan carnival. When the healthcare apocalypse hit her own term, which she uses just to annoy Blake, everything fun like bad food and booze was outlawed. In her opinion, there haven't been a lot of reasons to smile lately.

Still, the slightly overweight dandy with the expensive haircut and top-end jeans standing at the grocery checkout counter causes the corners of her mouth to curl into an unexpected grin. It isn't what's in his shopping cart: a collection of starch-rich breads, whipping cream, eggs, and other odds and ends. And it isn't his attitude: they way he smiles indulgently at the bored clerk, like a Mafia don excusing a family member who might be a little soft in the head.

It's his love handles.

The extra flesh rolls over the tight waist of his pants like an exposed secret, masked by his loose shirt, but not hidden. The shirt's fabric clings to its swell in a way that, she has to admit, is almost sensual. Her eyes trace along his meaty waist

49

in a furtive caress as she unconsciously compares it to Blake's almost skeletal torso, then climb to his face. There's a moderate bulge beneath the stranger's chin and a roundness to his cheeks that reminds her of a Caravaggio. Even his skin has a slightly reddish sheen, as if aglow from his lifestyle's excesses. How a man so obviously heavy for his frame can pass a biotag scan and be cleared to buy luxuries like whipping cream is beyond her. She finds it exciting, even dangerous in a way.

A package of vitamins falls from the counter to her feet, and she automatically stoops to retrieve it.

"Thank you," the man says.

His voice is a baritone, stroking the air rather than passing through it. As she stands up, she catches him staring straight into the dark cleft of her cleavage (naturally ample, despite the rabbit-food diet her biotag demands she eat), but it doesn't offend her. His dark brown irises are richer than any she's ever seen, and his silky black eyelashes, which tickle the tops of his plump cheeks as he blinks, shine as if wet. His long, straight nose is the only sharp aspect of his features, its point hovering over his deliciously full lips. Marla realizes she's staring, and feels herself blushing as she passes him the vitamins.

"You're welcome," she replies, having to swallow first to loosen her throat.

He smiles broadly, an expression so engaging she feels herself wanting to lean forward and taste it, running her tongue along his lips like a lollipop. Then he turns back to the clerk, finishes his transaction, and leaves.

"Ma'am? Your tag?"

She quickly shifts her eyes back to the clerk, wondering how silly her expression must look to him. Trying to conceal her embarrassment, she reaches out with one hand to let the young man pass a wand-like bioscanner over the band of biologically altered skin cells encircling her wrist. The device reads her health status and checks it against her purchases, then sends a message across the clerk's digital readout, clearing the sale.

***

"We've talked about this, Marla. You know you're prone to kidney infections. Drinking caffeine only increases the probability that you'll get another one. Do you want to live to be sixty or a hundred and ten?"

Blake came home early and began helping her put away the groceries. As he'd pulled her Kenyan coffee beans from the bag, the passive-aggressive admonishment began in the usual way, with a heavy, disappointed sigh and condescending cross-examination.

"I'm not a child, Blake. I wish you'd stop speaking to me like one."

"I'm just looking out for you. For Pete's sake, Marla, I'm the director of Age Infinitum's Health Sciences Division. It's my job to monitor biotags for every citizen in the Greater Atlantic Alliance. How does it look if my own girlfriend has compromised health?"

It's only Wednesday, right? And already, he picks another fight. She's hardly in the mood, still experiencing that giddy teenage lust directed at the man in the grocery store. Why does Blake always act as if she's incapable of taking care of herself? Why can't he just live and let live?

She closes her eyes and takes a deep breath, knowing that nothing she says will make any difference. When she opens them, she keeps her focus on the groceries, trying to avoid being provoked by the mannered offense in his expression.

"Just forget it. It's not even about me anyway. All you care about is your quarterly report and how many people Age Infinitum catches eating an extra helping of proxy chocolate. The more people your company gets kicked off National Health Division's health program, the more funding you'll keep getting. I told you; I'm not a child, I know how it works."

"Marla, really."

His lips keep moving, but her mind is elsewhere. She'll drink her coffee, and he'll be angry, but her biotag cleared it and he hardly has any authority to control what she eats or drinks, as long as it's legally purchased. God, it's like she's living with her father.

***

"I'm sorry, miss. It looks like you're not cleared for the steak, but we have a fantastic tuna and caper salad if you'd like."

"If I have to eat another salad I'm going to vomit," Marla says to Erin, her lunch date. Then to the waiter, "Fine. Can I get bleu cheese dressing?"

The waiter consults his scanner readout and smiles. "We have an excellent soy-cheese substitute. Will that be okay?"

"No. I'm allergic to soy. Just the balsamic vinaigrette." She knows it's not the waiter's fault that her family has a history of heart disease, but she wants to strangle someone, and he's the closest. Sensing the rising threat, the waiter quickly disappears.

Erin picks up the conversation they'd been having before their order was taken. "Really? He told you he thought you should start seeing a couple's therapist?" She takes a drink of water, trying to cover her pitying smile, Marla is sure. Her friend has heard enough of these complaints over the last two years, and she knows Marla won't do anything but gripe. "Just because you aren't going to give up coffee?"

"It's bullshit, I know. I don't need some quack telling me to make compromises for my own happiness." She pauses, waiting for Erin to dutifully agree and reiterate what a bonehead Blake is, but Erin only takes another sip of her water and looks past her at the rest of the lunch crowd. "Anyway, he's going on a work trip this week. Maybe he'll forget it if I don't bring it up."

"Maybe," Erin agrees, but there's no heart in it.

Damn, Marla thinks, *even my best friend can't hide how bored she is by my ridiculous façade of a relationship. Maybe it really is time to do something about it.*

She searches for something else to talk about, and the man from the market peeks out from her mental photo album, clearly impressed into her memory from her constant recollections over the last few days. "You know, Erin, I have to tell you about this guy—"

She's interrupted as the cautious waiter delivers their lunch. Erin's mind is elsewhere, and Marla decides to drop the subject. She picks through her salad with a predictable lack of enthusiasm, hoping Erin doesn't catch the envious way she can't help glancing at her waif-thin friend's roasted vegetable and tenderloin special.

Halfway through their meal, a disturbance in the foyer catches their attention, and they spot the vests of an Emergency Services crew hustling through a crowd toward the elevators.

"Wow, I wonder what that's about," Erin remarks.

"Let's see what's going on," Marla says, grabbing her purse and waving her credit card at the table reader, the insipid salad happily abandoned.

***

The show is over by the time they find a good vantage point, but the story wafts through the watching crowd like a morning mist. It was Edward, the new accountant for their department; probably an aneurysm; dead before he hit the floor; drug use noted as the cause. Sadly, his next of kin will never see a dime of death benefits. NHD won't pay out for self-induced death.

Erin nods with somber interest as the story is relayed, but Marla is barely listening. Her attention belongs to the stout paramedic gathering up medical equipment scattered over the office carpet. It's the man from the grocery store, his bulky form just as tantalizing in his blue tailored ES uniform as it had been the week before in his too-tight shirt and jeans.

He glances up and catches her staring. A wide grin spreads over his face as if he recognizes her, and she smiles back with what is probably too much enthusiasm. He's not the red meat she's been craving, but there is no ignoring her almost rapacious attraction.

Erin leans toward her, whispering, "Wow, obviously something wrong with that big boy's b-tag. Maybe someone should stop feeding..." But Marla's cold stare freezes the rest of her friend's commentary in her throat.

***

Red silk curtains keep the light and most of the noise from the street below from interfering with their evening. Two glasses of Primitivo absorb the muted candlelight, casting a wavering ambience over the embroidered tablecloth and remains of their five-course Italian dinner. Tony tells her the wine comes from the Mediterranean Federation, who have no sanctions against alcohol as long as citizens' production doesn't drop, and that he's able to get it through a relative who does a lot of international travel. She doesn't care how he gets it; it's the most delicious thing she's tasted since the NHD health regulations passed ten years ago.

It's been over three weeks since Antonio Lazzarani introduced himself on the same afternoon poor Edward the druggie accountant had collapsed. He'd been in the lobby of her office waiting for her after work. When she saw him through the opening elevator doors, she'd thought she was imagining him, her obsession grown out of hand, and her heart stutter-stepped before settling into a heavy-metal rhythm. Perhaps it was time to cut back on coffee after all. Then he was standing next to her, reaching out to take her hand, kissing it, and telling her she was more beautiful than Debussy's Clair de lune. Could he buy her an espresso or a latte? She'd nearly gasped in surprise, but it hadn't been that hard to say yes.

And the sex; the sex was more than good. It was fantastic! Explosive, passionate and robust, ranking high above the fondly remembered martinis she so missed. How could she have forgotten what good sex was like? That velvet fire that spread from her center and consumed her, even from something as small as his hands running along her back. The healthcare apocalypse had stripped more pleasures from life than just forbidden food; it seems to have made everything as dull as her diet.

Everything about Tony is the opposite of Blake. His lips are the perfect sweetness and texture of a ripe mango, soft and yielding, but with a hidden firmness that still makes her body feel liquid when they kiss. When she runs her hands along his arms or hips, it's like a treasure of flesh, the embodiment of opulence. There's a feeling of firmness to him, a real and touchable substantiality that no man she's known has possessed. He feels real and complete in the way that the others felt hollow and shell-like. And she can't get enough of him.

She's lost count of how many times they've made love since meeting, maybe fifteen or twenty, and she's sure Blake is suspicious. Something else she doesn't care about. Her mental litany of his faults, his bossiness, his needling, his egotism, his bony ass and hollow cheeks, fades into the background whenever she and Tony are together, and she barely pays attention anymore to Blake's not-so-subtle accusations. That part of her life is coming to an end, and she's one unprovoked criticism away from chucking it out for good.

As deliciously irresistible as he is, Tony has another attribute that makes her quiver with desire. He cooks, and cooks well. None of the pasty soy-protein-isolate breads and whole-grain goop that passes for nutritious fare these days. He makes something like manna: pastas swimming in cream sauces, chicken drenched in curries and spices, steak and desserts that are both as marvelous and forbidden as apples from the Tree of Wisdom. Her dresses are clinging more tightly than they used to, and the half of her bra collection reserved for the time of the month when her boobs swell up like puffer fish are the only ones she fits comfortably into anymore. She's just waiting for someone at the office to ask her if she's pregnant, and she knows she'll have to scale back these excesses soon, but for now, it's too much to resist.

And why should she? She's not a robot, not like Blake, doing what the NHD tells him without question. She's a person with her own tastes and desires, and she should be free to do as she pleases. No one is ever going to die because she loves crème brûlée. Shouldn't it be her choice to eat it or not?

Tony is into her too, she's sure. He wouldn't go to so much trouble to impress her if he wasn't, right? The fancy dinners, the secretive calls during the day when he knows she's working but can't, or won't, ignore him, and the unexpected flowers he's sent her twice. Yet, there's something nagging at her, a voice in her head that she's been quite successful at ignoring. The extravagant dinners are amazing, yes, no argument, but Erin had had a point. How could he buy any of it? He's heavyset, no way to refute it, and his biotag is a clear ribbon of darker pink skin around his wrist. With the NHD's healthcare reforms, no scanner in the country would let him buy cuts of marbleized steak or gorgonzola cheese. Which means he's getting these things illegally.

What is it about Tony and his delicacies that makes her not care? Is it really that everything tastes so much better now, after years of food that had all the variety and flavor of cotton balls? Or is it the memory of that freedom, the choice to eat or drink whatever she desires? And now that she has that again, how could she possibly give it up?

***

Blake had reacted exactly as she'd predicted: wounded incredulity followed by choleric histrionics. She'd thought calling her a "fat, frumpy slut" was going a little too far, but refused to stoop to his childish name-calling. Her suitcases were already packed, and it had been easy to slip out the door, calling back that the movers would be there on Saturday to get the rest. After two years of codependent pandering and dysfunctional doldrums, the most she expected to salvage of their relationship was the hope that he wouldn't change the locks before that.

A cool Atlantic rain shower accompanies her as she drags the suitcases to the XCity SkyTran, but she doesn't mind. The water beads lightly on her long hair, dripping playfully into the collar of her jacket and tickling her neck. It will give her an excuse to strip naked when she gets to Tony's and wait for him in bed. He isn't expecting her tonight, but after the last few weeks, it seems entirely natural for her to be showing up unannounced. If he minded, he wouldn't have given her the door code. They haven't talked about her moving in per se, but if it turns out that she's being a bit too presumptuous, she'll just stay with Erin for a while until things settle down and she has a chance to find her own apartment.

Tony lives in one of the older downtown buildings, one that still has an electric elevator rather than the newer magnetic kind. As it clanks up its cables, she notes for the first time the yellow-brown stains retreating into the dingy corners of the floor and the cracked plastic casing on some of the buttons. The old-world charms she's always imagined the building bore now look a little faded, a little seedy. This is the first time she's been to Tony's without him, and something about it doesn't feel quite as she'd expected. As if she's committing some personal transgression, like lifting up the edge of a theater curtain and glimpsing the actors without their makeup, old and wrinkled, tawdry, ugly, and false. She imagines what it would look like to Tony's neighbors, this strange woman they'd only seen a couple of times. Some floozy, invasive and cheap, like a creeping vine that you can't quite kill once it's laid roots in your yard.

The elevator shudders as it reaches the fifth floor, and the doors hesitate before opening, perhaps considering whether or not she deserves to be set free in this building that isn't hers. Finally, they telescope clear in a halting, mechanical slide. As she pulls her suitcases along behind her, the wheel of one catches in the gap between the doors and the floor, forcing her to yank it free, and making her feel as if the whole building resents her being here.

Shaking it off, she walks down the empty hall to Tony's and enters the door code, stubbornly resisting the belief that it won't work. The lock releases with a soft hitch, and she sighs, relieved. She's just overly emotional, upset after breaking it off with Blake. Only natural. It would be strange if she didn't feel at least a little sad about it. There should be some leftover béarnaise and crab in the refrigerator, and possibly a bottle of chardonnay. That will be perfect. She can wait for Tony in peace and quiet, maybe work on a little buzz, and let the residue of her and Blake's relationship slough away like old skin cream under a steam shower.

After rifling through the fridge for a minute, she gives up. He must have eaten it for lunch. He hasn't been to the market in a few days and nothing easy and quick to cook remains.

Perhaps there'll be something in the freezer she can reheat.

The icebox is like a miniature Antarctica, the frosty air that swirls out as she opens the door turning the rain still in her hair and on her neck frigid and uncomfortable. Packages of frozen shallots and phyllo dough block the front, and the door shelf holds equally unappealing items. She pushes the first layer aside and finds several more bags of frozen meat and vegetables. Almost ready to accept the idea that she'll have to unthaw something and cook it herself, she reaches to the back corner and comes across an opaque container, half a quart in size. Hoping it will be some kind of delicious dessert, maybe a chocolate torte or ice cream confection, she pulls it out and lets the freezer door swing closed.

***

"What the hell are those, Tony?" she cries as he walks through the door.

The stark container inhabits the tabletop between them, alien and accusatory. His eyes jump from where she stands near the drapes, one hand clutching anxiously at the still damp collar of her shirt, then follow her pointing finger to the container. She sees the way his expression freezes for a moment, then his widening eyes fly back to her face.

"I know what you must be thinking," he says, his tone as silky and soothing as a fine port. "But you have to let me explain."

There is no doubt that he does know exactly what she's thinking, what anyone would be thinking after finding a box of biotags that had obviously been removed from the arms of real people in their lover's freezer. What she wasn't thinking, couldn't bring herself to think about, was how they'd been removed, and from whom.

"Why do you have those... those things?"

He sets a shopping bag he'd brought in with him beside the table and walks to her side. He tries to put a reassuring hand on hers, but she jerks her arm away before he can touch her. The skin around his mouth and eyes sags in sadness.

"Please, Marla "

"Just for God's sake, Tony just answer me."

He sighs. "Okay. I'll tell you the truth. You deserve to know." Walking back to the bag, he begins pulling items out and laying them on the table, pushing the biotag container aside with no more ceremony than if it had been a napkin. "I use them to get things like this." He places a quart of vanilla bean gelato on the table. "And this." A set of bacon-wrapped filet mignons follows. "And this." He lifts a square box from the bottom of the bag and sets it next to the other items. Pulling open the lid, he reveals a cake with icing made of chocolate so dark she can almost smell the cacao beans as they'd roasted. "Your favorite. I got it to mark our first month anniversary."

His words catch her by surprise. Had it been a month? The time had slipped by so quickly, so many indulgences had accumulated, that she hasn't realized how long they'd been dating. But the momentary tingle of excitement she feels at this realization is trampled by the loathing she has for the question that has to be asked. "Wh–where did you get them?"

Instead of answering directly, he pulls out a chair and sits, placing his hands palms down on the table as if to prove he has nothing to hide. "When people die, Marla, their biotags retain a trace of energy, a static charge. Enough that the tags still work for a while. The difference is, when they're no longer attached to people, they can no longer read any personal bio-info. Do you see what I mean?"

She shakes her head miserably, trying to force the echo of the words *when people die* out of her ears.

"When you're dead, nothing can kill you," he explains. "So nothing is off limits. The biotags of dead people let me buy anything I want."

Her stomach lurches. "You cut these off of corpses?" It makes sense; he works for Emergency Services. He sees more death in a week than most people see in their lives, and she knows he is friends with the city coroner. "You desecrate their bodies!" she tries to scream, but it comes out a horrified whisper.

He balls one hand into a fist and hammers it down on the table hard enough to make the containers jump. For the first time, she sees anger in his face in the way his brow creases into a cascade of wrinkles, and his lips tighten. "Damn it, what's more of a desecration? The NHD forcing people to wear these bio-engineered manacles their whole lives, or letting people go to their graves in the same body they were born with? Don't you see? I refuse to live as a prisoner in my own skin. I've thrown off my chains, Marla." He takes a deep breath, and his expression rearranges itself back into the slightly chubby but undeniably handsome face of the Caravaggio she'd first fallen for. "I thought that's what you loved about me."

Inexplicably, the image of the salad she'd been trying to eat for lunch the day she'd met Tony comes to mind. The memory of the smell of its overcooked tuna and slightly wilted lettuce turn her stomach more than what he'd just said did. She realizes she hasn't eaten anything she hasn't wanted since she met him, and she's never been as happy as she has been in the last four weeks. Like he said, she feels free. For the first time in ten years, she's living on her own terms, making her own choices, and experiencing no regrets. What good are NHD sanctions that attempt to prolong life if that life is not the one you want?

She looks into his eyes and sees the same warmth and, yes, love, that she'd seen in them nearly every day since their first date. His gentle and compliant hands are flat on the table again, and she knows they will never harm her, had probably never harmed anyone. And that was the thing; did it matter how he got the contraband biotags? He wasn't hurting anyone.

She approaches the table, takes the seat opposite him, slips one of her hands into one of his, and asks, "Would you mind if we have dessert first?"

SWEET
SAM BUTLER

Sam Butler has been previously published in The Gettysburg Review, The Found Poetry Review, the Foundling Review, and others. In 2013 one of her personal essays received a Special Mention from The Pushcart Prize: Best of the Small Presses and a Notable nod from Best American Essays. After graduating from Knox College in 2013 with a BA in Creative Writing she moved to Texas, where she maintains a small but exuberant cactus garden.

Five years ago a couple of chemistry and psych majors from a small Texas university got together over a Bunsen burner, hoping to create some trippy new designer drug that would make the weekend doldrums a bit more bearable. Pot's passé, LSD's dangerous—I don't know what their reasoning was and I don't really care, either, because it doesn't change what they made. They tested whatever the hell it was on themselves. White rats are apparently too expensive for people dicking around with hard-to-find chemicals. One of the students sickened from a trial batch, and one of them lost most of the feeling in his lips, but no one was killed or reduced to a vegetative state. If someone had died right away things might've been a bit different for the rest of us, but that's stupid to think about. "What's done is done." Something.

Anyway, they found what they wanted in the end. I did, too, eventually.

I got a call from a guy named Mark at 3:00 AM on Tuesday. He used Charity's phone, where my phonebook entry name reads Charlie—beautiful bitch CALL IF DRUNK. Mark said Charity was at his place. He'd thrown a party and she'd been the last in attendance with no way home. I didn't bite his head off for waking me up the night before a major chemistry exam. This was about Charity. I put on my shoes, grabbed my cars keys, and asked for his address.

Mark lived halfway out of town in a gated community. He waited with Charity at the gatehouse. Charity sat hunched on the curb at his feet, hair framing her bowed head like a curtain. As I pulled up I watched Mark grab Charity by the elbows and tug, hard, to make her stand. Drunk, I decided, but then she walked the ten feet to my car without stumbling. Charity always stumbled when she drank.

"I think she might be tripping," he said when I got out of my truck, but I didn't respond as I walked to the passenger side. Mark and Charity trailed behind, her head still bowed as we shepherded her into the pickup cab and onto the black bench seat. When we got her in and buckled (a process she did nothing to speed, leaving her arms hanging wooden at her sides), he repeated, "I think she was doing drugs."

"Probably," I said, and because I was supposed to, "Thanks. For not just leaving her, I mean."

"Yeah," he said. I could tell he was tired and pissed behind exterior civility. I felt the same way, only I was also worried. Then again, I was always worried about something and it wasn't like this was the first time I'd been worried over Charity. Or Charity and drugs, for that matter. Watching her drop out of school and start using had sent my blood pressure on a steady upward climb.

"I'll get her home," I said as I walked to the driver's side. Mark hovered by the headlights like a ghost, body swimming in swirls of golden dust. "Thanks again."

"Are you sisters?" he asked. When I stared at him, one foot on the floorboards and the other on the pavement, he added, "I'd be pissed, having to come out this late."

I said, "I'm used to it." I got in the car so I could roll my window down. "Thanks again," I called. I backed down the driveway, craning my head out the window. My rearview mirror had fallen off months before. Mark had vanished by the time I looked back.

Charity and I grew up together. I was into paper-mache volcanoes; she was into crayons, and eating them. We lived three blocks from one another, well within the range of training wheels and scooters. We bonded on my kitchen floor while our mothers baked cookies. If we were good they promised to take us swimming at the local YMCA, and we were always good, though that was mostly my fault. Charity wanted to paint the walls with ketchup and dig up Mom's begonias to look for buried treasure. I hid the ketchup bottle and told her I was allergic to flowers. She put up with me because I was the only kid in a neighborhood otherwise filled with the geriatric. In the end we made a decent pair, I guess.

Charity was the creativity. I was the analyst. She took things beyond face value, searching for meanings hidden deep beneath layers of grown-up assumption and assigned value. A broken flower pot became a crown, a bug became a dragon. I was always the knight to her princess, the wicked to her witch, the too-literal thorn in her imaginative side. Still, despite my occasional inability to go along with her schemes, she never gave me up as a lost cause. "Then you can be the mad scientist," she'd tell me when I told her I didn't believe in evil wizards. "Go build a volcano to destroy the earth and I'll come blow it up, because I'm the good guy."

She never tried to make me feel like the bad guy. That comes from something in me.

Charity didn't blink when I said, "I have to be in class in a few hours, you know." Her silence didn't surprise me. Charity had never much cared for tardy policies. As I rolled up my window and took the ramp onto the highway, I added, "Can you hear me or are you too high?"

Her head lolled against the back windshield as I drove, a strand of hair falling between her parted lips as she smiled, smiled, smiled out at the lampposts and houses and cars flickering past. I didn't press her to talk. Her eyes found my reflection in the window and glimmered with recognition.

"Hi, Charlie," she said in a small voice. It wasn't quiet, exactly, or gentle, just small. I didn't have any trouble hearing her over the air bursting through my open window.

"Hi, Charity," I said.

She made a hollow puh-TOO noise, forcing the hair out of her mouth with her tongue and breath. "Hi," she repeated.

"How much did you smoke?" I asked. "Were you smoking?"

"I took Sweet," she said.

My vision tunneled. I think I almost drove the car off the road.

"I'm sorry, I think I just hallucinated," I said. My tone was playful, light, open; my chest felt tight, claustrophobic, crushed. "Wanna run that by me again?"

Innocence marked her. She said, "I took Sweet."

The chemistry and psych majors' drug starts by giving the user a burgeoning sense of calm, one that swells in the chest before bursting like a flood. Users find themselves feeling languid and at ease once that euphoric orgasm dies down. About an hour after initial consumption (time varying based on the user's weight and metabolism) they begin to smile uncontrollably. It's a reassuring sort of smile, not too big or too small or too creepy, a smile you'd expect on the face of a Buddha or maybe even Gandhi. Takers look around themselves with unerring composure, wondrously absorbing the sight of everyday objects as though seeing them for the first time. Everything seems to jive just right with their inner monologue. I've heard of someone starting to cry, overjoyed, at the sight of a spinning windmill.

Some takers hum tuneless songs that are hard to hear. None of them sing. If pressed, they will describe what they feel. They use the words "happy" and "content," but none of the users will ever start waxing poetic on the subject. In fact, it's rare that any of them even speak unless forced. They sit in silence, smiling and retreating into some private world from which they wake up in a short few hours. Once the process is over they shrug and tell you that you'd have to experience it for yourself, really, I don't think I can talk about it just yet.

The chemistry majors and psych students at that small Boston university named the drug "Sweet," because one of them said he felt that way, after.

"Why?" was all I could ask.

"Why not?" came Charity's response. Her fingers traced patterns on her jacket.

"That's not an answer."

"Why not?"

"Because it just isn't, Charity."

She hummed a little. She sat up straighter so she could peer out the windshield in fascination.

"I can see what's in your headlights, but only for a second, and then it's gone," she marveled. "The trees are there and then they disappear forever. If I'm not looking they don't exist."

Sweet is not addictive. There aren't any "users," or "junkies," or people with "Sweet-teeth" as the preachers and politicians used to say back when Sweet hit the market. "I learned what I needed to learn," most takers will tell people who ask if they crave another hit. Takers act as if by a combination of chemicals in a glossy red pill they discovered everything about life worth their precious time. "I'm happy now. I don't need more than what I've got. Stop asking."

I kept one eye on Charity and one eye on the road ahead. I asked, "How long ago did you take it? Can you throw it up?"

Charity's head lolled my way; she was scowling, the expression knifing through her Sweet-happy haze like a butcher's knife. "It's too late for that," she said.

"Won't know till you try," I said, readying a finger to shove down her throat.

"Like you'd know," she said, turning back to the window.

"What's that supposed to mean?"

She matched my question with one of her own. She had work to get the bleak words out through the web of Sweet.

"Where were you when I really needed help?" she said.

I stared at the road, hard. The yellow dashes marking the road's center glimmered before vanishing under the truck's left wheel. I imagined I was squashing them one by one, that every ten feet I committed murder.

"I don't need help now, Charlie," she said, voice soft and full of understanding. "But now that I don't need it, you want to give it more than ever. It's too late. You're too late."

Charity and I started kindergarten together, both sporting lunch boxes bigger than our heads and enough pencils to fund a small army of journalists. The Moms dropped us off with tearful kisses and squishy hugs but neither Charity nor I felt homesick or scared like so many of our classmates. We had each other, after all what was there to be scared of?

Bullies, for one thing, bullies and germs. I figured out I was more scared of the latter than the former, and then the former picked up on the latter, and then they were picking boogers out of their noses and chasing my neurotic five-year-old self around the playground like Wile E. Coyote after the roadrunner, only I wasn't fast enough to outdistance them every time. Charity was the one to go totally against her name and shove them back, screaming to leave me alone or she'd tell teacher, I swear to God I will, but whenever she wasn't around they liked to pick up where they left off.

The bullying continued until the first grade, when Charity gave one of the kids a black eye and said that if they told on her she'd karate chop them. Tae Kwon Do had made her tough. I think she learned it for my sake but she would never admit to anything.

I didn't know what to say. I settled on gripping my steering wheel as if it were trying to fly out the open window. My hands would have shaken otherwise. Charity stared out into the night and smiled, smiled as if our conversation and her accusations had never been voiced.

"I just don't understand," I managed a few miles later.

Her smile didn't waver when her head fell to one side, tapping against the window with the sound of a hollow coconut. Her face reflected darkly in the glass; the twisted image looked more like my Charity than the wraith in my passenger seat.

"You're not supposed to," she said, all dreamy and at peace and calm, and for a second I found myself hating her. "Poor Charlie."

"Poor me," I echoed.

The fact that Sweet does not facilitate addiction was the main reason it was not outlawed when it rose to popularity during 2020 and 2021, spreading happy smiles and quietness in its wake. It also helped that several senators of note tried the drug, believed in its effects, and quietly put down what few motions were proposed to make it illegal, or at least a prescription drug. It passed from hot-button topic to something as mundane as Tylenol with hardly a hiccup to impede its progress.

Sweet is an anti-depressant more effective than any in existence, said some.

Perfection is hollow without tasting Sweet, said others. Whatever that means.

"Where did you get it?" I asked after a few more miles whipped by. "Sweet, I mean."

Her smile grew. "A friend. A good new friend."

"Did you plan on taking it tonight?"

"No."

My mouth opened. Then it closed. "You mean you took Sweet on a whim?"

Her eyes were miles away when she said, "Of course not."

A part of me felt relieved.

"It's something I've wanted to do for a long time."

Those words would have killed me had I not been so intent on taking Charity safely home.

Our friendship confused people. Charity was the small spitfire of a girl with the beautiful face and black curls; I was the quiet one with mousy features and enough nerves to power a rocket ship. But she never abandoned me, not even when the popular girls tried to bring her into their fold and told her I was a nerd who should only merit disgust.

"Charlie's not so bad," she'd always tell them, sneaking a sideways glance at me. "Charlie's the smartest."

When they were gone she'd mimic one of their walks, or a particularly piggy face, until I laughed, and she said we should go play in the mud on the playground, because it had rained the night before and the worms would be out and wriggling.

I kept glancing at the fuel gauge. I hadn't checked it before running off after Charity; the needle hovered a little over empty but we still had miles to go. The prospect of getting stuck in the middle of nowhere with Charity in the Sweet state wasn't something I liked to think about. I pulled off the road at a truck stop to fuel up, telling her to wait in the car while I pumped. She didn't acknowledge me, eyes closed as she hummed nothings into the watery fluorescent lights under the gas station awning.

I figured I should get some food in her; it's what you did for drunks, so why not Sweeties? I had to do something for her, anyway; if I didn't I'd go nuts.

And I did go nuts. I bought a bag of pistachios, her favorite, and two cups of coffee. The cashier looked at me with a critical eye when I approached the counter. He said, "Hope you don't mind my sayin', but you don't look so good."

He wore an old Rockets jersey and he had skinny arms dappled with purple liver spots but I didn't see anything but fatigue, crassness, and just a little smudge of humane concern in his rheumy eyes. They lacked Charity's disturbing clarity. Good thing, too, because I don't think I could have handled that right then. I opened my wallet and carefully extracted enough crisp bills to pay for the food.

"My friend just took Sweet," I said. I immediately regretted speaking. My fingers twitched as I put my wallet back in my hoodie's pocket. The leather felt cold and slick, and then I didn't regret speaking anymore. I wanted human contact. I didn't care whose so long as it wasn't Sweet.

The cashier sized me up before making a face expressing sympathy. He slowly dragged the pistachios across the price scanner. "My girlfriend did it a month or two ago," he said, tone pitched low.

My breathing stopped, then started. "Is she different?"

"Yeah."

"But is she still… her?"

The cash register door opened with a pop. "No." He counted my change and held it out. "Yes. She's still her. Just…"

He faltered, pushing the door shut with a ping. I said, "Sweeter."

Charity changed after her parents' divorce but I think that's to be expected of most seventh graders. It's my fault, it has to be, were my grades not good enough, please make it all make sense, Charlie—I heard it all because Charity never showed how much it hurt at school, or in front of her parents, or in front of the people who could have stopped what happened next. It shouldn't have been me but it was me she came crying to, a kid who didn't know the first thing about handling depression or whatever it was that changed her. She wondered what she'd done wrong and how she could fix it. I watched her stop imagining and writing and drawing and start buying makeup by the pound. The cosmetics did little to hide the vulnerability she didn't want to show. We stopped seeing each other as often because she had to spend half of the year's weekends with her dad and his new girlfriend in another subdivision.

She got her first boyfriend in the ninth grade; I covered for her so she could spend the night at his house and lose her virginity on their second date. Skipping school, drinking, hurting herself in ways I tried not to think about, I'd be an idiot to discount drugs—she did things I would never do because I was too scared to break the rules for which she held nothing but disdain. I made excuses not to go with her when she invited me out to hang with her older crowd: They're so cool Charlie, they can buy alcohol and it's so fun, you should try it.

I probably shouldn't have avoided her. I guess I was too much of a coward to ask for a one-on-one sleepover, a reenactment of the play dates we used to have.

I watched her through the windshield, walking back to the truck slowly to buy us time we didn't have. Charity's silhouette stood out against the silvered glass like a stain; I saw her lean forward, breathe, and fog up the windshield with no trouble. She raised a steady hand and drew a star in the condensation.

Vapor rose from my cup of coffee, and for a moment I was blind and my hands shook.

Charity's star had faded when my vision cleared.

She ran away from home in the eleventh grade. Charity didn't show up for eight terrifying weeks, ones I spent becoming an insomniac and printing out missing-child posters, and when she did show up it was at a truck stop in the middle of Nebraska. She couldn't remember how she'd gotten there, only that she had been heading to Vegas with a caravan of new-age-Romani and that they must have left her behind when she took too long in the bathroom.

After that she dropped out of high school to wait tables. I stayed in town for college but the only times I ever saw her were when she got drunk and needed a ride home.

I put the pistachios on her lap when I got back in the truck. When she didn't move to open them I took the task upon myself, tearing the plastic bag with a crumple and pouring the nuts into my hand. I cracked one open, carefully placed the shells in a small Dixie cup I'd snagged off the truck stop's condiment counter. I held the naked nut out to Charity.

"Please eat it," I said, and she did.

She started crying. "It is so good," she mumbled into her hands. I tried not to scream at her to quit that, it's embarrassing, STOP IT.

Instead, I asked, "Why did you take Sweet?"

"Why not?" she said.

Sweet changes people. There aren't many who contest otherwise. The change is something you can see in their eyes, as recognizable as a burst blood vessel or a pulsing stye. It's a perfect stillness, the type I thought you could only find in the eyes of sages or priests on enlightenment's cusp. The look speaks of acceptance, of unyielding love, and of knowledge so vast the universe starts getting small.

I want to shatter that look.

Desperation made me shudder when I tried taking my coffee cup out of the holder below the radio. "What about your mom and dad?" I asked, taking a sip I didn't taste.

"What about them?"

I gaped. "What about..."

Her head rolled my way on a boneless neck but her eyes had slipped closed. She wasn't crying anymore. "They'll be fine," she said. "I'm sure they will."

"But if Sweet..."

Bright eyes opened. I wanted to punch her. "Everything will be fine," she said, speaking slowly, and then she chuckled with warm humor. "I've given them so much trouble."

"That's no excuse to kill yourself!" I said, stabbing my keys into the truck's ignition. I shifted it into gear with the engine roaring and slammed out onto the highway.

It wasn't until 2022 that the sudden rash of human disinte- grations tearing up the news networks and Sweet were linked. They called it "ashing," and they called Sweet unwitting self destruction.

The only ones who seemed to care were those who hadn't taken Sweet.

"You're going to die, Charity," I said, foot leaden on the gas. "Do you not understand that?"

"I was always going to die," she said. With firm fingers she rolled down the window and held her hand out into rushing dark. "Before Sweet and after, too."

"You chose this. Choosing death is suicide."

"You can't choose to not die," she said, hand out with fingers spread so the wind could pass over and through them. "No one wants to live forever. Who would want to live forever?" Her hand clenched into a fist, pushed back by the motion of the car until her elbow went taut. "You could die right now," she said. She pulled her hand back into the car and placed her other fingers on my knee, stroking. "Don't get angry. Don't worry. You can't control it."

I didn't say anything. I pressed harder on the gas. The speedometer climbed from 65 to 70. Her fingers dragged up my thigh and then pulled away.

"You could lose control of the car right now," she said in that sing-song voice. She huddled close to her window. "The brakes could fail and you could die. But you chose to get in this car, didn't you? You turned the key in the starter and pushed the gas. So your death would be a suicide."

I said, "That's different."

"Is it?"

The needle climbed to 80.

"Yes," I said. "Risk is living."

I've only ever seen one person ash. I was on my way to a biology lecture, thinking about the test I was going to take, worrying that I hadn't studied enough, barely seeing as I tumbled inside my head. Two people walked in front of me. I didn't notice either of them—I saw them but I didn't see them, the way you do with strangers—until the girl on the right stopped walking. The girl on the left took two steps and stopped. She turned back and asked, "Sarah?"

Sarah didn't move. She crumbled. Skin imploded into dark grey heat and cracked inward, bursting out in a shower of pale dust. No sounds, no flames, no hoopla or grand finale or trumpets blaring just ash that hit the ground long after Sarah's untouched clothes fell in on themselves, an invisible girl with garments too heavy to bear for another moment.

Sarah's friend (her calm friend with placid eyes that understood everything and shared little in return, Sweet eyes, eyes I didn't want to meet) stared at the dark pile for a second. Then she rummaged in her bag and snapped a picture with her cell phone, dialing the dead girl's mother, saying, "Mrs. Kane? Sarah ashed. Yeah, I took a pic. I'll text it to you. Bye."

I couldn't move. Sarah did. Her ashes scattered as the wind picked up and tossed her pale blue shirt across the sidewalk.

Charity, oblivious of the hair in her face and the air blasting through the window, said, "You didn't choose to be born. You didn't choose to take that risk. Your parents chose to make you, and you're going to die." She giggled. "Are they murderers?"

85 MPH, getting faster. "Shut up."

"So I'm going to die," she said. "I'm going to turn to ash, and I'm going to die. But you'll die too. The only difference is that I know how I might go. I'm going to explode and become a part of the universe. Death is now my choice."

Something inside me burst. "Why don't I just flip this car right now and see what kills you?" I ground out. The needle climbed higher: 90 and rising. "Is that risk better than your fucking certainty?" My hands shuddered on the wheel and for one dizzy moment I saw the image just as it would be: the skid of tires, the world tipping sideways as we flipped, the sky becoming ground when we rolled, the roof crunching in on us and smashing my head apart like a melon filled with red. Charity wouldn't scream, she'd just smile and welcome the oncoming black, but I'd scream, I'd scream so loud that—

Charity put a hand on my arm and I was crying. I took my foot off the gas and pressed the brakes, watching the red needle plummet down to 70 as we slid forward in our seats. At 50 I really started slamming, hammering away at that brake like it could save her life and mine at once. Charity's head snapped forward, bam, against the dashboard, and then it went back like her neck was made of straw, but she didn't say a word or cry out in pain. The gravel on the highway's shoulder made my tires skid but we didn't flip when I scrambled blindly for the keys and killed the engine, face pressed into the steering wheel so I could sob and not look at her while I did it. The din of the horn filled the dark as my headlights powered off.

There's no time limit on death by Sweet. There doesn't seem to be a connection between actions taken prior to ashing and the act of ashing itself. Some of the chemistry majors and psych students from that small university in Boston who took the first batch of Sweet are still alive today. Some probably will be for a long time. Some died within weeks, some after a year. I've heard of people ashing seconds after they take the pill. There have been cases of old people taking Sweet and dying of natural causes without ever ashing at all. A few have died in accidents before Sweet killed them. Not enough time has passed to tell if anyone my age can live a full life before Sweet comes for them, but people are trying.

Now Charity is one of them, I guess. I thought about that as I cried against the steering wheel. How long did she have? How long did I have to be with her?

Charity put her hands on my back and cooed, rubbing to soothe. It worked. When I finally felt I could look at her she was covered in blood from the face down, the dash had broken her nose. I took off my jacket and started blotting the red from her skin. The feel of denim on her freckles made her laugh, made my fingers shake. She took my hands and pushed them to her lap. She leaned forward and pressed her forehead to mine.

"Hey, Charlie," she said. She tucked my hair behind my ear, slicking my temple with her blood.

"Hi," I told her. "Hey?"

"Yeah?"

The answer, if there were one, struck me as stupidly simple, sadly simple. "Come over," I said. "Let's watch a movie.

Order pizza. Just… hang out." I swallowed and touched her sticky cheek. "Like we used to."

She giggled. She agreed. I don't know if Sweet made her pliant or if she actually wanted to be with me but that night she was mine again, the way she'd been when we were kids.

I knew I'd be hers until she stopped being anything at all.

GREENTEETH
ROBIN EAMES

Robin M. Eames is a queer beastie who likes weird art, folk things, and gnomes. Robin lives in Australia with a cat and several musical instruments. This story is probably not autobiographical.

Sinfi's mother bought the farm from a flat-eyed man with pale pink skin and a permanent sneer. It was late September and the weather was already getting cold, and the man said that this winter was going to be a bad one, and that they should go south while they still had the chance. Sinfi's mother didn't listen. People are always saying things like that to Sinfi's mother, because her skin is dark and her eyes are soulful, and they think that means that she's feckless and can't be held down, that she can't be trusted, that she came here to steal good people's jobs. Nobody ever remembers that Sinfi's mother's family has been around these parts for centuries, longer than some of the old village folk.

Sinfi's mother wants to settle down. She's got a horse and a rusty old plough, two cows, five geese, seven ducks, a dozen chickens and three pigs. The pigs are friendly, not dirty at all, and they have mottled hairy skin and wrinkly eyes. Sometimes Sinfi sits with them and listens to their happy gabbling noises and pretends that she can understand them. Pigs aren't difficult to understand, not like humans.

In October the leaves start to turn brown and orange and dead-looking, and by the end of November the trees are all skeletons rising up out of the mist, stripped of their pretty green jewellery. Sinfi feeds the birds and milks the cows and collects the eggs, while her mother goes out into the fields and plants wheat crops. They sell the chicken eggs in the market, but they keep the duck eggs for themselves. They taste better, and they're bigger. Sinfi isn't used to working on a farm, but she knows the value of hard labour, and her hands have never been soft like the village girls with their painted nails. By December Sinfi's muscles are getting almost as big as her mother's. It makes her feel strong, like she could take on anything. She'll turn eighteen in a few months, and she'll finish her correspondence course next year, and she can feel her future unfolding out in front of her.

The winter hits them hard. The smallest pig dies, and Sinfi's mother cuts up the meat and makes a hot pork pie with soft golden pastry, and she puts the rest of it in the freezer. The pig was Sinfi's friend, but she eats the pie anyway. They can't afford to let things go to waste. They keep the cows in the barn, because the snow's too thick for them to graze properly, and the frost freezes their eyelashes together. The barn smells like hay and horse dung. There are holes in the roof, so little bits of snow come drifting down through the ceiling to melt on the floor. It's still cold but the cows don't seem to mind too much.

Out near the boundary of their property there's an old aban-doned mill, and Sinfi likes to go out and sit on the crumbling steps and be alone for a while. Sometimes she takes a book, but when the weather's bad she just wraps her coat around her shoulders and stomps through the slurry of mud and melted snow, getting away from the farm, away from her mother, away from everything. The millpond froze over a while ago, and the layer of ice is so thick that Sinfi can jump up and down on it and it won't so much as crack. Shadows swirl beneath the surface, but the ice is clouded and Sinfi can only make out vague shapes. Sometimes she swears she can see fingertips pressing against the underside of the ice.

At night Sinfi clutches her blankets close, and counts her heartbeats. The wind howls like a dying beast, rattling the windows and shaking the skeleton trees. She wants to keep a light on, but they're trying to save electricity, and she doesn't need protecting from her own nightmares.

When the weather starts to warm up again Sinfi is relieved, because she'd begun to think that the winter would never end. Her mother doesn't say anything, but the lines around her eyes are looser, and she starts to smile and laugh again. Sinfi's mother has a weird sense of humour. She tells Sinfi not to stray too far into the woods, because there are monsters there that will gobble her up. Then she says that she's joking, because the real monsters are human, and she laughs high and loud like the cawing of a magpie.

Sinfi isn't stupid. Monsters are things that people invent so that they have a reason to be scared of the dark. Still, she rather fancies the idea, so for a while she goes exploring around the woods looking for gnomes and fairies. She doesn't find any, but occasionally she hears an eerie chattering carried on the breeze, and once she found a set of tiny little footprints in the soil, shaped like a person's but barely bigger than her thumbnail.

In the second week of spring, she meets Jenny.

The village is miles away, but there are a couple of little houses and huts dotted around the mountain near the farm, and Sinfi thinks that Jenny must have walked over from one of those. Jenny shows up one day knocking on the door of the barn. She was in the area, she says, and she wanted to drop by and say hello. Sinfi's mother is out at the market, but Jenny doesn't mind. Sinfi pours her a glass of milk, fresh from the cow, and they sit next to the pig-pen and chat about the wheat crops that they'll harvest in the summer. Jenny suggests that they start up a veggie garden. They've got the soil for it, she says, and it seems a shame to waste the space.

The pigs are weirdly skittish around Jenny, and the cows start an awful bellowing when she goes near them, stamping their feet and rolling their eyes around. They're not used to strangers, and it takes Sinfi a while to calm them down. She apologises, but Jenny just laughs, flashing teeth that are wickedly sharp and a bright blue-green. Sinfi blinks, and stares, but then Jenny turns and smiles at her, close-lipped, and she thinks that she must have imagined it.

Jenny comes back again the next day, and the day after that. She never does meet Sinfi's mother; somehow it never comes up. They go walking through the woods together, and Sinfi shows off all of her favourite places, the trails and meadows and tiny streams, and the huge old oak tree with glistening spider webs strung between its branches. Jenny seems to enjoy it, but her face is so smooth and slick that it's hard to read her expressions. Her skin is pallid, with an odd nacreous sheen, and her hair is thick and wild and dark. She's taller than Sinfi, with long gangly limbs, but even though she looks awkward she moves surprisingly gracefully, as if she's dancing. Her irises are pale blue, but her pupils and sclera are black as pitch. Her nails are long and sharp, like claws. She's beautiful, but it's a scary kind of beauty, like the sun. If you look at her for too long, it burns.

Jenny never dresses properly for the weather. Even though it's springtime now, it's still horribly chilly in the mornings and evenings, but Jenny only ever wears the same old tattered black dress. The fabric clings to her skin as if it's wet, and trails along the ground behind her but never seems to pick up dirt or stains. Sinfi offers to lend her a coat, but the cold doesn't seem to bother her.

Sinfi's never really had a proper friend before. They always moved around too much and too quickly for her to make any real connections with the locals, and now that they've got the farm they're too far away from everyone else to make friends. Anyway, the villagers disapprove of her family, and her background, and her clothes, and the way she does her hair, and it's hard to befriend anyone who gets hung up on stuff like that. Jenny is different. Jenny's sort of a space cadet, actually; she doesn't keep up with the news, or with recent technology, or films, or books, or anything. She likes fairy tales, she says, and Sinfi buys a copy of Grimm's Hausmärchen and reads it from cover to cover.

When Sinfi is with Jenny she feels like her heart is about to flutter out of her chest like a bird. The whole world feels brighter, filled with a sweet and unearthly light, and Jenny's green-toothed smile is the centre of the universe. To be the subject of Jenny's intense attention is dizzying, hypnotic, and Sinfi falls in love almost without realising it.

I-love-you becomes a secret phrase breathed between them, hung between their lips, wandering over their skin. The words are magical, but not because of any inherent special meaning; rather they are powerful because they resonate, echoing all the times the phrase has been uttered throughout history. Every time Jenny whispers I-love-you, a thousand fairy tale princesses mouth the words along with her; a thousand famous lovers touch fingers between bars; a thousand literary heroines sigh and clutch flowers to their hearts. Sinfi is intoxicated with love, and for once she has found something outside of books that feels vibrant and addictive.

The darkness leaches away with the dawn, and, slowly, as spring progresses, the nights become less lonely and less frightening. Jenny's eerie gaze strips away all of Sinfi's unspoken fears and doubts, and her clammy, bittersweet kisses sweep every other thought out of Sinfi's love-addled mind.

They meet by the millpond every morning, and Jenny weaves tiny white flowers into Sinfi's hair. They read poetry to each other; Sinfi reading Wordsworth and Jenny murmuring in a language that Sinfi doesn't recognise, a language that fills her ears with a distant roaring, that makes her blood throb wildly in her veins. Sinfi presses cold kisses to the underside of Jenny's bony wrists, and Jenny clenches her claw-tipped slender fingers and stretches her mouth out in a vicious grin. Her gaze is ancient and knowing.

Sometimes Sinfi arrives early, and she stares at her reflection in the water, and almost thinks that she can see Jenny's pale face staring back out at her. Jenny's hair fans around her like seaweed, and her eyes are black and endlessly deep, and her smile has sharp edges. She beckons, and Sinfi moves closer to the water, breaking the surface with hesitant fingers, reaching out for someone that isn't there.

Good morning, says Jenny later, sitting down beside Sinfi and dangling her bare feet in the water. Were you waiting long?

No, not long, says Sinfi, and stares into the millpond as if it contains all the secrets of the universe.

Spring slides into summer, and eventually it's time to harvest the wheat. Sinfi's mother arranges to borrow a big creaking combine harvester, and she spends a couple of hours inspecting the engine for dust and dry crop debris before she's happy with it. The tires are enormous, and when it rolls along it makes a huge, angry, rumbling sound, chewing up the wheat with sharp metal teeth. The raw, earthy wheat-scent is heavy in the air, accompanied by the tang of hot metal. The heat of the day seems like a tangible thing, settling around Sinfi's shoulders like a cloud-tipped cloak.

As the weather gets warmer, Jenny's mood seems to sour. On cloudless days she flops around on the mill's stone steps like a beached fish, all waxy skin and wide, desperate eyes. Her movements are slower, more languorous. Her speech is slurred. Often Sinfi arrives to find Jenny already reclining in the millpond, fully clothed, with her arms curled through the spokes of the waterwheel and murky algae tangled around her body.

Sinfi asks if there's anything she can do to help, but Jenny just snorts and sinks further into the water.

These days Sinfi always feels a step out of sync, like the world is ever so slightly out of alignment. Very gradually, her connections fall away; the heat of summer doesn't even reach her, and worldly things like the blue sky and the burning fields seem detached and distant. The world feels unreal, or maybe it is Sinfi that is unreal. Something within her is changing, transforming. She longs for darkness, for the cool, damp, peace of the millpond. She longs for the comforting chill of Jenny's arms wrapped around her, the soothing not-poems whispered in her ears. Jenny herself is lazy, languid; her blue-black eyes flicker in the waning light of dusk, and her every expression seems deeply seductive. She is different in the summer, more approachable, more familiar. It only makes the rest of the world seem all the more foreign.

When autumn comes, Jenny speeds up again. She is faster, sharper, brighter, and everything else seems slower and duller in comparison. Sinfi spends more and more time lying by the bank of the millpond, dancing her fingers across the surface of the water. She doesn't bring a book anymore. Instead she stares into the depths of the millpond, into the depths of Jenny's inhuman eyes, into the depths of her own unknowable soul.

She abandons her studies, her chores, her old life. She doesn't feed the horse, or milk the cows, or collect the eggs, or sit with the pigs listening to their nonsensical squealing. None of that matters anymore. The only time she feels true peace is at the old abandoned mill, watching the ripples in the water, watching the reflection of the sky create a new internal universe just for her. She is changing, she knows. She is no longer indifferent to the heat; it stings her skin, and hurts her throat. The sclera of her eye is darkening, and her teeth are growing sharp, even a little green.

Sinfi's mother watches her constantly, now. The lines around her eyes are tight and unhappy, and she often tries to coax Sinfi to eat something, to read something, to go outside and get a little sunlight. They have several screaming arguments before Sinfi's rage just falls away, and her mother, like everything else, becomes dim and grey and unimportant.

On the first day of autumn, Sinfi takes her shoes off and leaves the farm, sinking her toes into the cold earth. There is frost on the ground, and the wind is biting. The coming winter is going to be a bad one.

At the millpond, Jenny is waiting for her, and her eyes are huge and black and loving. Her smile is sweet, and her lips are the dull colour of the algae that gathers in the pond, and her teeth are the bright blue-green of the water lit up by sunlight, almost glowing. She beckons.

Sinfi takes a step forward, and then another, and then she falls into Jenny's arms, feeling the water wrap around her. She breathes in, and the water rushes into her throat, and Jenny's eyes are luminous in the dark.

THE RUIN
SARA NORJA

Sara Norja dreams in two languages and has a predilection for tea. Born in England and currently settled in Helsinki, Finland, she is pursuing a PhD in English linguistics. Her poetry has appeared in publications such as Goblin Fruit, Curio, Strange Horizons, Through the Gate, Plunge Magazine, Niteblade, and Interfictions. Her short fiction has appeared in 365 Tomorrows and Quantum Fairy Tales, and is forthcoming in the anthology An Alphabet of Embers. She blogs at http://suchwanderings.wordpress.com.

The forest breathed green around the two travellers. They had passed from tightly clustered greenwood to an area where sunlight reached the ground, unchoked by dense foliage. The path they trod was free of undergrowth, no longer the mere guess of a trail it had been deeper in the woods.

Andanu raised his eyes from the tree-rooted path to examine his teacher Taril as she trudged ahead of him. She was tireless, never bowed down under the weight of her travelling pack, her eyes constantly keen and interested in the world.

He had slept poorly and his back ached. He trudged along behind Taril, leaning heavily on his staff with every step. He envied her light strides. They had left their small west-shore town a week ago, and he felt the day's weight on his shoulders. He hoped they would get enough new patrons at the east-shore town's great summer-festival to make the journey worth it. At least the way through the forest was the shortest way from coast to coast of the island, even if it was a foot-wearying, bone-aching way. Most people preferred to take sail and skirt the coast eastwards, but that would have required funds that Taril and Andanu did not have.

Before they left, Taril had hummed songs that spoke of great trees, of lands swallowed up by the great green, of the mystical experience that was the forest. During their journey, Andanu had discovered that he appreciated the majesty of the greenwood better from afar, when he didn't have to sleep on tree-roots every night.

"Do many travellers come this way?" he asked to get his mind off the line of pain tracing its way along his lower back.

Taril glanced back at him, eyes crinkling in a smile as she beheld his no doubt peevish expression. "Not as many as used to in the old days, so they say," she said. "But yes, this is a common route. Particularly used by rogues and musicians-itinerant such as ourselves." She didn't stop walking, although her pace relented a little, and Andanu was able to catch up to her. "Of course, nothing is as it was in the old days."

"The days before the great smoke?"

"Just so. Those days three hundred years past and more. Do you remember the song I taught you, about the faces in the green?"

"Yes." The first line, *As I wandered in the wilds*, slipped into his head, and he knew he could sing all nine verses if needed. He was pleased to discover that even the more obscure songs stuck in his memory these days.

"That song is ancient. They sung it in the days before the great smoke, if our musician-sages guess right." Taril's steps slowed down, irregular. "We have such precious little knowledge surviving from before. All we have are a snatchful of songs and tales."

Andanu thought about how much there must have been to know in the old days. The thought made him shudder at the vastness of it all. Perhaps it was a blessing, after all, to live in a later age, a simpler world.

"Wait!" said Taril suddenly. "What's that?"

The hair on Andanu's neck stood up. They had been fortunate enough to encounter few dangers on the road so far; his skills with his fighting staff had not been needed. Most of their encounters had been with fellow travellers eager to accept their gifts of music and tales in return for food and a

94

fire. Still, he took a firmer grip on the staff now.

Taril had wandered off the path to the left. Andanu followed her among the mossy trees and riotous undergrowth.

They pushed past an ivy-covered oak and discovered themselves in a small glade. It was thrown into shadow by two immense trees on the other side. Gnarled and knobbly-barked, they reached towards each other, their branches weaving together so seamlessly it was as if someone had made them so. They formed an arc, almost like a massive gate. Andanu chuckled: the forest was making him fanciful.

"This," said Taril, her eyes narrowed, "hasn't been here before."

"What do you mean?"

"I've walked the forest path before. This glade has not been here."

Andanu raised his eyebrows. "Sounds like one of your ancient tales. Perhaps you just haven't noticed this place before."

"No," said Taril. "I saw the sun glint on stone, just now. I would have noticed such a thing before." She pointed. "There. That's what I saw from the path."

Next to the huge trees, nestled near their roots, stood a ruined building of grey stone. It had once been a cottage, but the roof had caved in and all that was left was its bare outline. The doorway gaped open to the skies.

"Why would someone have built a cottage this deep in the forest?" asked Andanu. He shook his head, trying to clear it. There was a strange feeling in the glade, as if they had stumbled onto a forgotten pocket of the land, where the memory of the past wove a strong spell.

"It shouldn't be here." Taril stalked closer to inspect the ruin. Trees had taken refuge in what had once been the inside of the cottage: they had grown tall, pushing up above the crest of the crumbling roof. Moss and ivy clung to the stones. "It's old," she said, "very old. Could be hundreds of years."

"You think this was built before the great smoke?" Andanu wandered closer, feeling tendrils of wonder creep inside him.

"It could be. This isn't how we build our houses. And see how tall and thick the trees are, growing within its walls."

Andanu scrambled over mossy roots and reached the grey walls dappled with fronds of ferns and moss. The stones exuded a coolness that was welcome in the rising heat of the day. He leant closer, touched the ruined door-lintel with his bare hand. "I wonder who lived—"

His head was spinning so fast he felt sick. He could feel his left hand still touching the cool stone of the cottage, but the real world was fading, and another reality taking over...

...and he spins into the cottage's memory. A confused jumble of images hits him all at once. A woman in a tall headdress is kneading dough on the kitchen table. The door opens, a man comes in with bow and arrows and a bunch of dead partridges. She runs forward to kiss him, takes his face in her floury hands. Many people run, laugh, die in this place. Children run clattering on the dirt floor. A homecoming fire burns in the hearth. The air is filled with the sounds of a great feast. Laughter, kisses: the cottage has known such things. And then the great smoke comes. How can it be anything else? Fire rages in the sky. Noise like thunder. Rain falls with the fire. Ashes, ashes. The roof burns down, the cottage screams as only stone-wrought creatures can. Andanu feels its pain as if his own flesh is burning...

He returned to consciousness with a jolt, hand jerking free from the stone. Taril's hand was on his shoulder. "What's wrong, Andanu? You've gone all grey."

He blinked, trying to focus his bleary eyes, and backed away from the wall. He fought against an urge to heave up the remains of his breakfast. "I saw something, Taril. When I touched the wall... I saw things. Things from the past."

Taril led him by the arm and sat him down on a knee-high root sprawling from one of the strangely arched trees next to the cottage. As he described what he had seen, he saw the frown lines deepen on his teacher's face.

He took a deep breath to steady himself. "The old tales I've learnt are full of magic, Taril. So much magic it feels unreal to us. What if the world was a different place then? Maybe things that are impossible for us might have been possible then, and some of that lingers in this place."

It sounded far-fetched even to him, but there was still a roiling pit in his stomach and black spots danced behind his eyes when he closed them. He did not doubt he'd truly had the vision. He was fairly sure he was not inclined to insanity, either.

Taril frowned. "You mean that those charlatan Magicworkers who swindle the gullible might once have truly been able to change the substance of the world?"

"Perhaps. Perhaps we've stumbled on a pocket of the old magic. I know it sounds impossible, but I truly saw the history of this place through the stone."

Taril snorted. "You're saying magic is tied to place? That's not what the Magicworkers say. They say it depends on the position of the stars and the deftness of their finger-work." She shook her head and reached into her travel pack. "There. That'll help with your queasiness." She handed him a piece of travel bread to gnaw on.

Andanu chewed on the bread. The bland taste did help quell the nausea. "I'm just spinning a tale, Taril. You know me." Yet it did not feel like falsehood.

Taril's eyes dimmed with thought. She looked up at the vast girth of the tree they sat under, her eyes tracing the branches where it joined with the other tree. "It's an interesting notion, of course. What if magic truly had once been part of the weave of this world? What if the tales we tell weren't so beyond the realm of the possible?"

"You're what-ifing a lot," Andanu said to goad her.

"Far less than you were a moment ago."

He felt hollow and fragile inside. He focused on the ruined cottage again, barely believing that simply touching the wall had forced such a vision on him. Could there truly be places in the greenwood where magic still coursed stronger through the veins of the world?

Taril took her flute from her pack and started to play a lilting tune that cut right into the heart. Andanu thought the tree-root he sat on trembled, an almost imperceptible movement. The leaves above rustled and sighed with many sharp voices even though there was no wind in the glade.

A shiver ran down his aching back. It was as if the tree was listening to Taril's music, dancing in time to her tune.

THE GYRE
REBECCA SCHWARZ

By day, Rebecca Schwarz is a mild-mannered editorial assistant for a scientific journal, by night she writes science fiction and fantasy stories. Her stories have appeared in Interzone, Bourbon Penn, and Daily Science Fiction. She is currently writing her first novel.

"The Gyre" previously appeared in *The Colored Lens*, issue 7, Spring 2013

In the middle of the Pacific Ocean the Gyre turns in a great lazy whorl. The current carries with it the trinkets of civilization: bottle tops, cigarette lighters, barnacled gym shoes, and Ziploc bags clear as jellyfish. Lost fishing buoys trail tangled nets, which in turn haul their unintended catch of dead fish, shredded Mylar balloons and schools of water bottles.

She spent her days collecting the most unusual items as they drifted past. Her hair, dark as kelp, brushed against her powerful cetacean tail as she moved through the water. She carried the things she found in a little flock of plastic bags. Plastic was all around her in various states of degradation. Their original shapes transformed under the agitation of the waves into a confetti that caressed her with its tendrils as she passed, decorating her hair, sliding past her shoulders and breasts, her hips and tail.

She hung the bags off her elbows and moved through the crystalline sunlight. Adrift, they looked ephemeral, but inflated with seawater they felt heavy, solid. Her favorites were the ones with the big red letters. The words on the bags said:

Thank You.
Thank You.
Thank You.

Earlier that day she had found a plastic doll, naked and missing an arm. She'd seen dolls and parts of dolls before, but this one was different—a miniature man. He rode in the bottom of a bag along with a pink, plastic flip-flop and a round container top decorated with the face of a pig-tailed girl.

She stopped, fished the tiny man out of the bag and looked into his still perfect face. Biceps stood out on his remaining arm. Bifurcated legs grew from his hips like the arms of a starfish, except bulgy and muscled like the rest of him. His limbs were jointed like a crustacean. She tried to put his legs through what she imagined was a walking motion and giggled. They must look ridiculous, these creatures, stomping around on land.

She hadn't noticed the boat above, as a pod of whales had recently passed overhead, but its shadow lingered. Rising, she saw a long pole with a small net at the end reach into the water and scoop up a glinting potato chip bag. The pole receded into the sunlight and disappeared beyond the edge of the boat.

She drifted closer. The pole returned, trolling through the water for another item. She searched her bags and pulled out a toothbrush with bristles so curled it looked as if it were facing into a strong current. She pushed it toward the seeking net, which scooped it up. As the pole retreated, the silhouette of a head and broad shoulders leaned out and over the boat's edge. A second head appeared, and together they examined her gift.

She lurked in the shadow of the hull and watched them collect more items from the Gyre. She could just hear their voices, wavering and garbled, punctuated by staccato laughter.

Day faded to evening, but the ship did not leave. Only after the first small points of starlight appeared did she break the surface to get a better look. Lights twinkled along the mast. The bags drifted around the crooks of her elbows. She held the man-doll in her hand, not wanting to lose him. The ship's engine gargled quietly as it had throughout the afternoon. The slick taste of diesel lingered in her mouth.

Three people moved about the deck talking and laughing. The man with the broad shoulders poured a dark liquid from a bottle into plastic cups the others held. She swam closer, keeping her head low in the water. He picked up a curved container made of fine wood and began moving his hands across the strings stretched along its length. She drifted along with them, enthralled. The sounds were both complicated and soothing. The notes progressed forward, then circled back as if to find something that had been left behind.

When she was a child, living among the vast estates of junk the merfolk collected in the bioluminescent twilight of the deep, an old aunt would put her to bed in a broken Plexiglas yacht that rocked on the sea floor. She told stories of the people who walked on the land: how their lives were comically short, but, in exchange, they possessed a soul hidden away inside them. Instead of turning to sea foam when they died, their souls would live on forever.

She asked her aunt how she knew this, and her aunt replied that long ago one of them had fallen into the sea and that her sister, the girl's very own mother, had eaten it.

"The human?" she asked, incredulous.

"No," her aunt laughed. "Just his soul. The rest of him she left for the fishes."

At the time she believed this explained her mother's absence, which none of her relatives would discuss. She remembered being immediately jealous, thinking her mother now possessed an eternal soul. But the old woman explained that, no, she didn't have it -- because she had eaten it.

She wanted to know where these souls went when they were through with the bodies they'd inhabited, but her aunt was impatient by then and claimed neither to know nor care, and that, in any case, she'd heard that men's souls weren't very filling.

Before leaving her alone in the sunken boat, her aunt soft-
ened and told her that, according to legend: a wish you make
after eating a person's soul will come true for as long as the
soul survives within you. She lay awake for hours that night,
thinking of all the wishes her mother might have made.

The people battened down the boat, tittering and unsteady
on their feet. She watched their silhouettes, trying to imagine the souls confined within them like the fish swimming
obliviously inside a net before it's hauled up. When the
people disappeared below deck, she sank beneath the surface
and slept, drifting and dreamless, trailing her bags of trea-
sures, which she'd tied around one wrist.

The next morning the ship was out of sight. She swam in
concentric circles hunting for it. Clouds covered the sun, and
it took some time to pick out the outline of the boat against
the gray sky. She started for it, but stopped when she saw
him below her. He'd attached large fins to his feet and a tank
to his back. Wobbly bubbles trailed up behind him. Curly,
golden hair floated freely around his facemask. She watched
his legs kicking languidly, separately. He too collected the
objects that floated all around them, choosing a plastic bottle
and a shredded vinyl purse. Her aunt had told her that people
only took living things from the ocean.

She descended and crossed his line of sight. He stopped what
he was doing and stared at her with an intensity that made
her skin flush. She continued sinking into the dim cool
below. She knew that her kind could attract people. Had
her mother attracted her sailor so? Her heart pounded as he
turned and followed with a kick. Then he pulled something
from his belt and trained a powerful light on her. She threw
her arms up too late; the beam left a purple smear across her
vision. Frightened, she turned away, powering her dive with
strong strokes of her tail. The light made a halo around her as
she swam through the dark, wavering tunnel of her shadow.

The light faded and she turned, hoping he hadn't broken off the chase despite her fear. He floated above, the light now pointed away from her face. She swam closer. Without taking her eyes off him, she reached into her bag and found the little man, holding it up for him to see. He moved the light to it and, with a kick of one foot, drifted closer. His eyes, through the mask, moved from the doll to her face.

He pointed to it then to his own chest. She nodded, as the current drew them together. He reached out and let some of her long hair flow through his fingers. When he exhaled, bubbles danced between them. They drifted along together for some time. He handed her the light and kicked his legs out in front of him so that she could inspect them. She reached out and touched the end of one of the flippers. He bent his knee and took it off, revealing a pale foot decorated with five little appendages, like fingers only stubbier. She laughed with delight. Replacing the flipper, he smiled, releasing more bubbles.

Tentatively, he ran his hand past her hip, feeling the thick muscle of her tail. His eyes filled with disbelief and delight. She reached up and traced the line of his jaw with her fingers. She held his gaze until he took the thing he used to breathe out of his mouth and kissed her. His mouth was warm and tasted of rubber and salt. She dropped the light then and pulled him to her. She thought of the soul hidden inside and thrust her tongue deep into his mouth. He responded, caressing her neck and breasts before wrapping his strong arms around her waist. When he broke away his eyes were unfocused, but he didn't take them off her.

Below them she could just see the light's beam slowly careening away, but he didn't seem concerned with that. Putting his breathing device back in his mouth, he pointed at a gauge on his wrist, then toward the surface. He held out his hand. She took it and they started up. It was a fair distance, and they moved quickly.

She watched him as they swam up into the light and thought of her mother and the sailor, gone so long now she was hardly more than a fairy tale herself.

This man was so strong and fine. She couldn't imagine he could possess something so delicate it would not survive inside her. She decided that she didn't want a wish, especially a wish that wouldn't last any longer than it took to digest a meal.

He stopped swimming. His hand clenched hers painfully, then he began thrashing. She grabbed the straps that held his tank and hauled him up, kicking with all her strength. They ascended, slowly at first, then gained speed, racing to the surface.

They breached in a spray of foam. White-capped waves collided with each other, and rain pelted them. He spit the thing out of his mouth with a wheezing gasp. She pulled his mask off and dropped it into the sea. After some fumbling, she unhooked his tank and let it fall away too. Now she could pull him easily, his head resting against her shoulder.

With each swell they rode, she scanned the sea for his ship. At last she spotted it bobbing in the waves. She pulled him along while he labored to breathe, his eyes bloodshot and unfocused. He tried to kick but could no longer control his legs; instead they bounced stiffly against her tail in a motion not unlike that of the articulated doll.

By the time they reached the boat he was groaning softly. The other two were on deck scanning the water. When one pointed at them, she ducked under and pushed him closer, falling away as his friends hauled him aboard.

They told him he'd been in the hyperbaric chamber for three weeks, but it felt like he'd been on this narrow bed his entire life. Every time he looked through the double-paned window he was surprised to see a generic hospital room on the other side. The only difference between the room he was in and the one he looked out on was the pressure and the concentration of oxygen. The other room had a chair, usually empty, his, a gurney.

He slept as much as possible to dodge the suffocating claustrophobia that pursued him when awake. It wasn't the confinement of the chamber, it was that he still couldn't feel anything below his waist. Propped up on an elbow, he looked down at the soft sheet, and the topography of his legs under it. With every day that went by, the sight of the still firm muscles of his legs felt more and more like an empty promise. The doctors couldn't say, in such a severe case of the bends, when, or if, his legs would come back.

Because they never turned the fluorescent lights off in the room on the other side of the chamber, the time he spent awake and the time he spent dreaming fused together. His dreams of the Pacific Garbage Patch were always the same. A blueprint for how things should have gone. He collected samples, and took pictures for Planet Neptune's Clean-Up Campaign. He never dove too deep, never rose too fast. But also, he never discovered her.

The campaign was just a tax shelter for the amusement park. When the narwhals he'd captured died and the animal rights people got involved, the park's management exiled him to the swirling garbage patch in the middle of the Pacific. Just until things cooled down, they promised.

He'd spent two months in the North Sea hunting the small whales. They were going to be a real moneymaker for the park. No aquarium had ever kept a narwhal alive in captivity and Planet Neptune spared no expense building a large, beautiful tank. Still, the mammals stubbornly refused to survive. After languishing only a few weeks, they died within twenty-four hours of each other. He'd begged management to let him hunt down another pair, but they sent him to the Gyre instead.

In other dreams she would join him in the chamber, long green hair flowing over full breasts. Her narrow waist widening into the sinuous tail, its flukes trailing off into a gossamer membrane. He would float free of the bed and swim around the small room with her through twisted fishing nets, mateless shoes, and drifting medical equipment. Barnacles attached themselves to the walls. Millions of plastic nurdles filled the seawater like a bloom of plankton, the little, round beads tickling his ears and drifting into his nose. He pursued her until he caught her up in his arms, then held her and kissed her, his tail twined around hers.

She was more real to him than the nurses and specialists who appeared randomly to draw blood or check his vitals, who told him they were scraping something sharp across his feet, or that they were wiggling his toes.

They could do nothing for him, but that didn't mean he was useless. He would find her and put her in the gorgeous narwhal tank at Planet Neptune. The park had many ways to acquire specimens, but when they wanted something from the sea, he had always been their man. He couldn't imagine a more sensational exhibit. With her in the park, no one would doubt his ability.

The next doctor who arrived to check on him found him sitting up with his legs dangling over the side of the bed. He told her he was ready to begin rehab.

She cleared him to leave the chamber, fitted him with a streamlined wheelchair, and moved him to a room with a window that looked out on a pristine lawn punctuated by an ellipsis of three scrawny ginkgo trees. He spent his days strapped into various weight machines working on his arms and core. In the evenings he swam laps in the hospital's clear pool that stank of chlorine, grabbing great handfuls of water, pulling himself forward, towing his legs behind him.

Back at work, he pulled on his old wetsuit and proved that he didn't need the use of his legs to scrub algae off the tanks. He took the swing shift, rolling in at sunset, maneuvering around the last sunburned, cranky families as they left Planet Neptune. He crushed popcorn containers and plastic cotton candy bags under his wheels. Grackles quarreled over french fries strewn across the paved paths. Every trashcan vomited crumpled food bags, sticky cups, straws, and diapers. A child's swim goggles hung from one can. Swarms of bees hovered, feasting on hidden pools of warm soda.

In his spare time, he quietly prepared the abandoned narwhal tank. When it had become clear the whales were dying, management cordoned off the path to the exhibit. Now, the only evidence that they ever existed were their spiral tusks displayed in the gift shop over a basket of narwhal plush toys.

The tank was beautiful, with a coral reef painted on the back wall and a faux-rock outcropping rising out of the water in the middle. From there the mermaid would be able to look across the park, down past the suburban rooftops, all the way to the shimmering Pacific.

While he worked on the tank he imagined hunting for her among all the things people threw away. He would take her from the sea, lifting her into the boat in the narrow canvas sling. On the trip home, he would smear lanolin on her tail and spray her with seawater.

Management knew of his extracurricular activities, but for now his chair bought him a lot of leeway. He intended to use every bit of it. One evening, just as he was pulling himself out of the water, his friends appeared, climbing through the small door that opened onto the molded plastic beach of the exhibit.

They had spoken a couple of times since the accident, but

never about what had happened to him out in the heart of the Garbage Patch. He scooted himself up to his chair, pulled himself into it and told them both everything. He could see they thought he was crazy, but it didn't matter as long as they agreed to his plan. He'd said, "humor me" and let them believe that it would help him accept his new condition. He assured them he just wanted to go back for a look, so that he could put it all away.

They took Planet Neptune's other boat, the one with the sling for transporting marine mammals, and set off for the Gyre. The trip went just as he imagined. He didn't dive alone this time. His friends had promised him three days, but the mermaid turned up on the second, a dozen grocery bags hooked on each slender arm.

She swam right to him and pulled out the same one-armed G.I. Joe doll she'd shown him when they first met. He moved to her slowly, carefully concealing the hypo until he was close enough to inject the tranquilizer somewhere around what would have been a thigh. She jerked back, her eyes wide with surprise for just an instant before she began to drift. He caught her in his arms, and they hauled her to the surface.

As they got underway, he busied himself making her comfortable, keeping her tail moist and picking bits of plastic and nylon fibers out of her long, wet hair. The others buzzed around behind him, taking pictures and oohing and aahing in disbelief. When her bags fell away in the water, he managed to grab the doll. Thinking it might comfort the creature, he laid it in the sling next to her.

They docked in the middle of the night, covered her with blankets, and paid off a couple longshoremen to help haul the sling to their pickup, then paid them a little more not to ask any questions. He sat in the truck bed between her and his folded chair, turned the blanket down and tucked it under her chin as they drove up the hill to the aquarium.

The man's head hovered over her, silhouetted against the night sky. He combed his fingers through her hair and spoke to her soothingly in his language. An engine roared in her ear. Her body, dry and sluggish, was wrapped in something scratchy. Whenever they rolled over a bump the ridged floor jolted against her back.

When they finally came to a stop, most of the stars had faded into pale morning light. The man pulled the blanket off her and scooted away. Someone she couldn't see pulled her by the tail, out of the truck bed and through a small doorway.

She twisted, clutching at the smooth slope to slow her descent. The little doll skittered down after her. Two people disappeared through the doorway, closing the door behind them; then the relief of the water rushed over her. The doll floated overhead. She grabbed it and looked around the small enclosure.

The crude image of a coral reef decorated the smooth wall behind her, but most of the tank consisted of thick glass. She looked out at a gray path that followed the curve of the glass. Beyond that two low slabs of wood flanked a large round container. The water smelled stale and dead.

The other two from the boat walked along the path stopping at the center of the window to look in at her. One sat on one of the wooden planks. Then the man joined them in a curious chair with wheels. He gripped the rims with his hands, turning them to roll the chair along the path. His legs didn't move at all. She clutched her doll and looked around; her bags, all the things she'd collected, were gone. Except for a tower of rocks in the middle, the tank was empty.

In the beginning, the man appeared in his wheeled chair with small groups of men and women who all wore complicated, formal clothes, the men in dour colors, the women in tight skirts that made their bottoms look like tails until the fabric ended at the knee and revealed their dual legs.

111

Soon, more and more people crowded the path, fat and thin, old and young, some carried babies or rolled them along in little canvas seats. All day they passed by, talking, laughing, and arguing. She had no idea the world contained so many people. They wore hats to shade their faces and held small, metal boxes up to the glass, which released bright, white flashes of light. One boy turned the thing around and, leaning over the railing, held it up to the window. The box held a tiny image of her floating alone in the empty tank.

She and her one-armed doll looked out on them. They drank from bottles filled with dark or bright liquid, used plastic spoons to shovel shiny blue sludge into their mouths, and dug pink fluff out of clear bags with sticky fingers. Others munched on greasy, brown sticks or loops that they carried on paper saucers. They ate and drank all the time, stuffing the empty wrappers and bottles in the round container until it flowed over. They put other things in the container too. Things she recognized. Had he brought her here to show her their origin? The things she collected in the Gyre, they were just the worn out shells of what people consumed with such abandon.

She missed sleeping in the little Plexiglas boat. Since most plastic liked to float, the things she brought home would rest against the ceiling over her bunk, twinkling as they jostled each other in the gentle, constant motion. If only she could climb out of the tank and choose a few items, for company, but the high walls of her enclosure were impossible to scale. When she could bear to look no longer, she swam in endless circles around the tank grazing the glass with her shoulder and fin until the sun set and the crowds thinned then disappeared. Tonight, a child's shiny plastic sandal lay on the path, bright yellow and tipped on its side, the shape of a flower imprinted on the sole. She wished he would bring it to her.

He pulled himself through the little door every night with a bucket of mackerel and slid down the slope to join her in the water. The fish were already dead and a little stale but edible. Every night after she ate, they struggled awkwardly up onto the rock in the center of the tank, she with her tail and he with his useless legs. Once settled, she would lean against his broad chest and listen to the melody of his voice, looking out over the trees and housetops all the way to the sea, waiting blackly, the stars above unable to touch its surface.

He avoided her tank during operating hours, didn't want to try to plow through the crowds that clogged the path, didn't want to see her looking out at him from the other side of the glass. In the evenings, when he wheeled past the last stragglers leaving the park, almost every kid clutched a plush toy mermaid. Management had ordered thousands in three sizes with dark green hair and shiny fabric for her tail.

Still, he could see she was not happy, alone in her tank, nice as it was. The exhibit would be better with a pair. His return to the Gyre, to find a companion for her, had already been approved. If there was one, there had to be more, he reasoned. Management would give him everything he needed: boats, equipment and a crew. In the meeting, the suits went on to discuss timelines and schedules, brainstorm events for the park, but he'd stopped paying attention. The hunt was the hunt. It would end when he captured another of her kind and no sooner.

He picked one of the plush mermaids off a spin rack on his way to her tank. It rode along in his lap next to the bucket of fish as he rolled up the path to her exhibit. In the water she held the G.I. Joe and the stuffed mermaid together in one hand while she ate. She looked almost human, the way she always chewed with her mouth closed, but he didn't think it was manners. It just made sense underwater.

She took longer than usual, eating a couple of fish then swimming around with the toys before returning for more food. She wrung all the air out of the mermaid's stuffing so that it would travel underwater with her.

His arms got tired sculling so he swam over to the rock and hung on, legs dangling below. Finally, when she finished her meal, she swam up to him smiled and held the mermaid toy up squeezing the water out with a wheezing hiss. He reached for it but she pulled back, her smile vanishing.

He climbed up on the rock and waited. Eventually she joined him, her narrow back warming his chest. A nearly full moon rose to preside over the sky, its light bouncing off the ocean below. He ran his fingers through her now clean hair, and explained that he would be going away. He told her he wouldn't come back until he'd captured a companion for her, maybe even a mate. He knew that was a long shot and he'd told them so at the meeting, but everyone agreed that acquiring a breed pair for the park would make Planet Neptune the hottest ticket in the country.

She sat, petting the little mermaid where it lay limp and sodden in her lap. Finally, she seemed to lose interest in the toy and tossed it in the water where it disappeared into the darkness. She slid in next and swam around. With only her head above the surface, she could be just a woman. She turned to him and lifted her arm out of the water, delicate fingers splayed, beckoning. He rolled off the rock and splashed into the water. She drifted away, arm still outstretched. He swam to her.

When she pressed herself against him a jolt from his lifeless bottom half surged up through his chest. He flushed. He hadn't kissed her since that first time in the Gyre. He'd wanted to, but it hadn't seemed right now that she belonged to the park. And she hadn't shown an interest, until now. What the hell, he thought. He'd be on his way to the Garbage Patch tomorrow. He dipped his head, brushing her cheek with his lips until he found her mouth. She responded like she had before:

deeply, searchingly. She swung her arms around his neck and they sank together, tumbling gently through the black water.

Eyes closed against the darkness, he kissed her as long as he could. Only when the air in his lungs was spent did he try to pull back. She responded by wrapping her arms around his shoulders. He tried to get a hand up to push her away. She locked her hands behind his back. Arching back, he could just make out her eyes in the dimness, unfathomable and predatory. He coughed and inhaled, stars burst in his field of vision. She held him patiently. Her mouth found his one last time, and she pushed more water from her lungs into his.

She drifted down with him until they came to rest on the bottom. After the struggle, his soul rushed into her filling her like the bright balloons bouncing on the strings tied to the wrists of the children who walked by the window.

She bobbed up to the surface remembering her aunt's fairy tales and made her wish. She couldn't imagine her mother wishing for a pair of legs, but she wanted to go home and couldn't think of any other way out of the park.

She lost track of time then, the pain was so great, but it was still dark when she swam to the landing area using the curious scissor kick she'd seen him use in the Gyre before his legs failed him.

She stumbled out of the water, clambered up the slick plastic beach and found the little secret door in the wall unlocked. She climbed down and began to walk toward the sea. Each foot swung out in turn and slammed into the ground, every impact reverberated up her spine, jarring her head. The landscape bounced sickeningly.

She cut across the park's maze of paths, tracking downhill straight toward the sea. The pavement scraped against the tender bottoms of her feet; in the grass, sticks and gravel stabbed them. Gasping in the cold predawn air, she lumbered ahead one foot at a time as fast as she could, her progress excruciatingly slow.

She fell to her knees at the gates and crawled under a turnstile. Even as the sky grew bright in the east, her eyes were failing. His soul dissipated, already tenuous inside her. Taking it had been easier than she thought, but she could not keep it. Still, she didn't think her body would consume it so quickly. She understood now that there would not be enough time.

She thought of her aunt, who raised her, shooing her every night into the little boat that rocked at the bottom of the sea. Who complained and pretended she did not have time for her, but always stayed to tell her one more story. Her aunt, down under the Gyre, who wanted nothing to do with the people of the air.

Hands and feet numb now, she stood and limped across the empty parking lot. A row of dusty oaks blocked her view of the sea. The last thing she felt was the warmth of the salty tears that ran down her cheeks as she dissolved into a puddle of foam at the edge of the lot.

Later that morning, as the sun reflected off the cars in their ordered spaces, a plastic bag tumbled across the pavement and over the little puddle of foam, which clung to it for as long as it could, until it dried, releasing it to the breeze. Plumped with air, the bag floated up and continued its inexorable journey to the sea and to the Gyre forever turning inside it.

And the words on the bag said:

Thank You.
Thank You.
Thank You.

ANOTHER YOUNG GIRL

ERIN KENNEMER

Erin M Kennemer studied creative writing at Texas A&M, though they deny any responsibility. She writes science fiction and fantasy, paying special attention to the weird and worrisome. Erin has received various awards for her short stories, including an honorable mention in Writers of the Future.

Ash lazily drifted to the ground, building up in piles a few feet from the smolder to watch the show. The village burned, and no one was alive to stop it. The smell of sulfur and burnt oil joined the stink of smoke, turning the air to vile fumes. In what had been a bustling town, only one structure stood, literally, on two metal chicken legs. The house began to root in the ash like a pecking fowl, until it found a nice bit of rot to settle on.

With a pop of grinding gears, the house let out a gush of smoke and sat. It breathed its satisfaction, fanning its windows like feathers. The red front door creaked open on steam hinges.

Miles away, deep in the forest, the White felt it. The damage to her domain sizzled into her flank, like a brand. She howled, sending the maggots scurrying away from the body beneath her. The White sprang from her dinner, trails of drying blood oozing from her muzzle.

The White flew like the winds of a storm towards the forest's ache. She reached the tree line bordering the scorched earth. Her eyes feasted on the dreadful house, and she longed to take claw and tooth to it. But where the ground burned she could not tread.

A black picket fence uncurled and planted itself in a square around a sprouting garden of black, twisted roses. Heads flew from the upstairs window and planted themselves on the spikes of the fence. Their jaws fell open, and they cried in unison:

Mountains and rivers and fields do not slow her,
Any Man be accurs'd to know her.
Baba Yaga Comes.

This village had revered and respected the White, and now it lay in wreckage. She could not tread where the forest was kept back, but there were other ways. She needed to find another young girl.

***

"What's it like living so close to the forest?" asked Gregory, his face pinched with envy.

"I guess it's not any different from living in town, except mother never lets me play in the back of the house," replied Mila.

"I bet you've never even gone in, have you?" said another boy from her class, Franz.

Mila didn't like the tone the conversation was taking. It was nice to have attention sometimes, but it always seemed to turn to teasing. Would they be impressed by the time she'd run in and out? They'd probably just tease her for not going farther.

Mila hedged. "My dad trades with Taiga village, so he goes in the forest all the time."

She made the right call. The boys crowded around her, looking impressed.

"Has he seen the White?" asked Gregory, leaning in too close.

"Well, no…"

She was losing their interest.

"But he's seen the bodies that the White leaves to warn off poachers."

School was long over and the sun was setting before Mila could break away from her new admirers. Her dad was due back from his latest trip, so she hurried home.

But her father wasn't there, and he didn't come home the next night, either. By day three, it was clear: her father was missing. The forest wasn't kind to those who were lost.

The pale blush of dawn on day four saw Mila standing at the edge of the forest. She had only moments to make up her mind before her mother would be awake.

Mila thought about her dad's soft smile and quiet voice and took a step forward. She remembered how her father had taught her to tell a good deal from a bad deal and took another step. Thoughts of his kindness and wisdom carried her deeper through the trees than she had ever been.

Soon, the path turned into a vague suggestion, and Mila became unsure of which way to go.

"Hello," said a grey cat, lazing on a rock.

Mila recoiled in surprise, but decided it would be rude not to reply. "Hello to you, too."

"You're not supposed to be here."

"I'm headed to Taiga. Please, just let me pass."

"The White demands an audience of all trespassers." The cat looked excited. "You're not a poacher, are you?"

Mila replied quickly, "No! Please. I'm just a little girl."

"Oh." The cat licked his paw, then sighed. "I'm afraid it isn't up to me. You'll have to see the White."

Mila choked up, despite herself. Large tears rolled down her cheeks and splashed onto the ground. Where each one hit, a small blue flower bloomed. Dread filled her. Had the entire forest grown from the tears of little girls?

"Interesting," said the cat. "Follow me. And don't try to run.

The White loves a hunt."

The grey cat led her to a large den. Bone shards were as plentiful as leaves, and the stench of death sweetened the stagnant air.

"We will wait here." The cat settled on a stump.

It didn't take long for the White to arrive. It was the size of five men, and moved with impossible litheness through the thick forest. The White bared its teeth, revealing bloody fangs.

The cat turned to Mila and spoke. "Her Majesty says she will let you go if you complete a task for her. You are special, more pure of heart than any other, and you will save your father." He sounded almost bored.

Mila rode on the back of the White and couldn't help but smile. She wished Gregory and the others could see her. The world was a blur of gold and green and black.

The White came to an abrupt halt, and Mila almost went flying over its head. She was about to ask why they had stopped when her eyes focused on the field in front of her. Instead of grass, the ground was black and charred. If this was supposed to be Taiga, something terrible had happened. Where were the golden buildings and bustling shops? Only one building was left, and it trembled slightly, like a slumbering animal.

She slid off the White's back, afraid to go any farther. Had her father been here when this happened? The White nudged her forward. Her foot hovered over the beginning of the char.

When she stepped down, a small patch of grass bloomed where her foot landed. As she walked, she left small boot prints of life across the emptiness.

Everything was so desolate. All hope left her. She wasn't going to be rescuing her father. Would she even recognize what was left of him? Tears fell freely, and she kicked at the stupid blue flowers that resulted. Maybe it was because she stopped walking, but the White growled at her back. There was no running away. There was nowhere else to go but into the wicked house.

As she got closer, Mila noticed a stream of smoke exhaling from the windows. On the roof, a weather vane tracked her instead of moving with the breeze. The worst thing by far was the fence, though. Mila let out a scream as heads mounted on spikes along it burst into song:

Mountains and rivers and fields do not slow her,
Any Man be accurs'd to know her.
Baba Yaga Comes.

She tried to ignore them, though she was filled with fear. Tears splashed down her face quicker, sending droplets flying as she scurried to the gate. One tear hit a head, causing it to explode in a bouquet of delicate blue flowers, its eye sockets now elegant vases, its mouth silenced by the blooms.

Mila pushed open the gate, trying to ignore the empty post beside it, room enough for one more head. The lawn was filled with thistles and brambles that cut at her ankles. Drops of her blood grew pink roses that choked away the black thistles.

The front door had its own set of carved teeth. It snapped its jaws as Mila approached. The handle of the door was a waggling tongue inside of the wooden mouth.

Disgusted, Mila walked to the nearest window and tried to peer inside. Dark ichor covered the glass. Mila tried to pry it open, but it was locked. A shutter whacked at her hand like a tail swatting a fly. She backed away.

"Hello?" She wasn't really interested in meeting whoever lived in this house, but the White had promised her father would be here.

She stood still so long, the mouth in the door calmed, hanging slack. Had it forgotten her? Maybe if she was fast enough, she could grab the handle.

Her hand shot out, grabbing the surprisingly soft knob, which twisted freely. The door swung open, but not before the teeth took a bite out of her. Her blood gushed out, and the door screamed, shattering into a thousand dry leaves.

She whimpered, putting pressure on her wound. The room before her was covered over in junk. The ceiling was a nest of jars hung from strings. Shards of broken glass and twisted metal winked at her from along the walls.

"Oh, let me guess, you're the plucky young girl of note and legend. Blah blah blah."

Dressed in red from head to toe stood a woman who appeared not much older than Mila. Her hair fell past her shoulders in a black sheet. Her smile was too wide.

"I'm looking for my father."

"Of course you are. How was your trip through the big bad woods?" The strange woman whispered something to a small wooden doll in her arms before setting it down. "I worked hard to get things ready."

"You're the witch! Why did you do this?"

The dark-haired, ageless woman laughed, a tinkling and mocking sound. "I'm getting things ready and harvesting hearts. I appreciate you bringing one straight to the door. I could have done without the property damage, though."

So, the witch wanted Mila's heart. Huge tears rolled down her cheeks and bloomed into ivy at her feet.

"Stop that this instant! What a mess. And who cries that much? I watched you walk up here. Waa Waa Waa. Why even come if you are so scared? I've almost certainly killed your father by now."

Mila let out another sob. "I had to try."

"Don't be dense. You're here because the White made you come. I see that damned beast lurking on the edge of my clearing." The witch took a step forward after giving a commiserating smile to her doll. "So, how are you special? Is it the flower thing? Are you pure of heart or some other such dreck?"

Mila fell back, trying to keep distance between them.

"They told me I was beautiful once." Madness had overtaken any beauty in the witch's face. "They told me I was special."

Mila spun around to run, but the witch grabbed her. Her strong arms pulled Mila inside and threw her on the ground. The woman pinned her, and Mila struggled to get free. Something caught Mila's eye, stilling her. In the kitchen, her father was tied to a chair, his head lolling to one side.

"Father!" Mila cried.

"Really? Huh. Don't get your hopes up, though. It doesn't mean anything. You aren't the heroine in this story."

Mila felt the air go out of her and looked up in confusion. The dark-haired woman had an elated look on her face. It wasn't until Mila saw the knife that she realized what had happened.

Blood began to pool out of the wound in Mila's chest, the knife still in place. It poured forth onto the floor and painted rivulets across the room. With the last of her strength, Mila smeared her blood across the witch's face.

With satisfaction, the White watched ivy explode from the house. She called to the ivy, and it grew towards her like a charging river. As the first vines touched her paws, she burst forward, using them as a bridge through the rotten field.

The front of the house was open, like an exposed neck. The White pounced. There was hardly room to move inside, and the White could only fit halfway in. The witch clawed at vines wrapped around her throat. Her whole body was engulfed in the new growth. Her hands sprouted flowers whose roots cut through her skin like a stitch through cloth.

The White bit the witch and shook her back and forth, until she laid still, then dragged her from the cabin. Her corpse tasted rotten, so the White spit it out.

And so Baba Yaga was defeated by the sacrifice of a girl as pure of heart as she was empty-headed. The White chewed on a bit of ivy, trying to get the dead-witch taste out of her mouth.

"I found another human in the house. You won't believe this, Majesty. I think it is actually the girl's father. I thought I was lying when I told her she'd save him. I've untied him, but all he can do is weep over the pile of flowers that she's become."

The cat spoke like a human and laughed at death. It made the White feel polluted. She growled, causing her servant to back up.

"I'll smooth things over, Majesty," the grey cat said with contrition.

After a while of hushed conversation, the father emerged from the house and sat down, holding his head in his hands. The cat gave the White a sly wink.

"And from this day forward, every time a blue flower blooms, the little girl is looking down at you. The little girl's-"

"Mila."

"Mila's last wish was to protect the forest. The End."

A laugh rose from the corpse of the witch. It was echoed by the heads on the fence. The White hunched, ready to fight.

"What will you do without a storybook maiden to throw at your problems?" said the corpse on the ground, its head twisted completely around. "Baba Yaga is here!"

Movement caught the White's eye. A huge hand gripped a tree at the clearing's edge. The tree withered and died. Another hand shot forward, grabbing the ground. The creature pulled itself into view.

It walked on two legs, like a human, but one leg was metal and hissed as it hit the earth. The grey hair on the creature's head was long enough to be woven into robes that hung loosely around its form. It closed the distance quickly, seeming to grow larger all the time. Its face was that of an old woman, but its nose was so bulbous, it looked snout-like.

"Majesty," said the grey cat. "I believe that is the real Baba Yaga."

"Then who was defeated?" cried the father.

"Just another lost maiden," gasped the corpse, a manic smile on its purpling face.

DAUGHTER OF THE SUN

A.E. ASH

Once upon a time there was a nerd who wrote books and poems about magic, mayhem, pew-pew and space and she lived awesomely ever after with her hubby and only mildly nefarious felines.

Something was buzzing at irregular intervals. Lian counted the electric metallic pulses. One-two-three, one-two, one-two.

One-two-three-four.

Not-quite darkness shrouded the communications cabin. Complete darkness would have been more comforting.

Lian Leandros stood, long arms hanging awkwardly at her sides. Flickering console displays cast the stains on her uniform into sharp relief.

How long had it been since everything had gone to, what was it they called it, hell?

"Hell." She said the word aloud. It felt clunky and foreign on her tongue. Ackerman, chief scientist in the Micro-Bio labs, had once suggested (loudly) that she "go to hell." One of the techs, a woman with a wide, mild face and an easy smile, had had to explain it to her.

"It's where people go to be punished for the bad things they did in their lives. I think it's a stupid old fairytale," the woman had said with a dry laugh before turning back to her diagnostics.

Hell, a place of torment. A Moebius strip of pain, a forever-darkness.

Lian's people trusted in the Forever-Light.

So am I here, where Ackerman said he wanted me? And is their hell such a thing as this?

129

"Here" was a violent then silent realm, a broken shell thick with the stink of fried circuits and flesh.

Ackerman was right. She was in hell and she deserved it.

How long has it been this way?

Lian counted under her breath. Shock had stuttered her sense of time so she tallied again--at least five Consolidated-standard days plus a smattering of hours. She wandered over to the main terminal and glanced down at the chronometer on the screen in front of her.

Five days, six hours and thirty-nine minutes, according to the display. Somehow, the malfunctioning instruments still kept accurate time. Lian surprised herself with a croaking laugh.

Absurd.

She lowered her hindquarters onto the cup-shaped metal chair crafted for bodies unlike hers and hunched her bulk over the transmitter.

She looked down at the input keys and hissed a soft curse. She'd lost the gloves she normally wore to make navigating Terran instruments easier.

Probably in the lab and covered in blood.

And now the holo-controls were offline. She focused and reached out. Tap-tip-tap, deliberate and stilted, the sound of her close-shorn talons on the keys. Instructions flashed before her.

[SYSTEM ACTIVATED. PLEASE BEGIN OUTGOING TRANSMISSION.]

Lian paused.

[PLEASE BEGIN OUTGOING TRANSMISSION.]

She spoke, slowly and with care. "I am Doctor Lian Leandros of the Consolidated Terran Scientific Research Team, Auxiliary Branch Xeno. I transmit to you now from The *Aldebaran* over all known frequencies. The ship is disabled and I require emergency assistance. If you receive this message, please respond. I will be here."

The backlighting on her console flickered, and static ripped through hidden speakers. Lian felt the muscles of her face tighten into what would be a fierce scowl amongst her kind. Probably horrifying to any Terrans who witnessed it, sharp-fanged and too wide-mouthed for their liking. Not that any of them were left on The *Aldebaran*.

[TRANSMIT MESSAGE AND END PROGRAM?]

Lian fought to think.

I cannot even say it. I cannot even say how it is my fault.

"I am Doctor Lian Leandros, transmitting from The *Aldebaran* and I...Oh, never mind. System? Please send my prior transmission at regular intervals over all frequencies." Lian winced at the waver in the words, a tide of disgust washing over her.

She sounded tired. Weak.

She'd come to hate her voice since she'd journeyed into Consolidated Terran space. Being among those so unlike herself for the past years made her aware of its imperfections. Too thickly accented for most Terrans to comprehend. Too alien.

And by her people's standards, hesitant, deferential.

It was the only living voice she had heard in, how many days?

"Ah, yes. Five." And of course, a smattering of hours.

She slumped in the comm chair, legs and tail stretching out over the floor until they were lost in shadow. Display lights cast a pall over the hide of her shaking hands. She realized with a jolt of dread that she hadn't checked in with The *Aldebaran*'s S.I. since the event. She curled her fingers over the metal of the console's edge.

I do not want to hear this.

Lian turned and faced the S.I. terminal on her left. Staring into the retinal scanner, she remained still until a flash of red nearly blinded her. Her eyes were different than theirs, the Terrans. Larger, thin-lidded and more sensitive. Lian blinked away the pain.

[CODE REQUIRED.]

She again spoke haltingly, keeping her long tongue behind her teeth.

"I am requesting *Aldebaran* ship intelligence emergency protocol, authorization LeandrosXeno3."

A sparkling ding of identification recognition rang in the air. A tiny, pleasing sound that made Lian feel, irrationally, like she'd finally done something right.

A computerized voice hailed her, only slightly distorted. "The *Aldebaran* S.I., Emergency Mode is online. Welcome, Dr. Lian Leandros. Would you like a status report?"

Lian didn't reply. The polite, androgynous voice eased her nerves, soothed her hearts to beating more slowly than before. The Terran language did not seem so brusque in the S.I.'s easeful voice.

Lian stared at her hands. Strong and fine-scaled. Cut, bruised. Blood stained the furrows of her fingertips and crusted the base of her talons. She fought to calm herself.

"Dr. Leandros, your pulse has increased over 15 percent from only 47 seconds ago. Do you require medical assistance?"

"No. I am merely ill at ease." Lian spoke so quietly she could barely make out her own words.

And there is nobody here to assist me.

"As you wish. I will continue to monitor your vital signs and issue instruction as needed."

"Thank you, Aster."

Lian liked the name Aster. She'd read about it, an old Earth flower named after an ancient word for "star." It seemed appropriate. Simple and violet-blue, the same color as the guiding star over her homeland.

Her own chosen name, Lian--to a particular sect of Terrans it meant "daughter of the sun." Those same humans could never hope to pronounce her true name, the name her people had given her. That thought always saddened her.

Leandros she'd chosen simply because it sounded like music.

Be one of them, she'd been told over and over before leaving for Consolidated Terran space. They will accept you more easily that way.

They will be less afraid of you.

They didn't understand that she was nothing to fear.

Only what I brought with me was worthy of fear.

That day she had stepped foot on the docking station serving as the gateway to Terran space, Lian had decided she'd become timid and harmless, because that was what they needed her to be. The healer, tame and mild, whose name was a sweet little word, not the series of whistling hisses and growls she'd answered to her whole life: "She Who Will Shine With The Fierce Light Of The Life-Giving Mah-tothi Sun And Who Will Aid Her People In The Forever-Journey Towards The Forever-Light Which Shepherds Each Star And Soul To Its Highest Destiny."

A better name, but not easy.

"Would you like a status report, Dr. Leandros?" Aster repeated, this time quieter.

"Yes. That is, yes please, Aster." Lian corrected herself then realized it didn't matter how polite and humanly she presented herself to be. Nobody else was listening.

"As you request, Dr. Leandros. Current status of Consolidated Fleet cutter The *Aldebaran*: All systems critical. Alarms disabled at your prior request. Fires in all sectors suppressed. FTL Drive status: catastrophic damage. Propulsion engines at zero functionality. Environmental controls failed in all sectors except for one and two. Artificial gravity failing in all sectors. Environmental controls in sectors one and two critical. Communications at negligible functionality. Less than seventy-two hours until auxiliary power fails in all sectors. Oxygen at--"

"Aster."

"Yes, Dr. Leandros?"

"Are there other life signs--" Lian couldn't say any more. The words stuck in her throat.

"Only one life-sign registers. It is located here in the starboard communications cabin. Yours, Dr. Leandros. With systems damage, I cannot know if there are others, but statistically it is unlikely."

"Of course. Thank you."

Of course. A strange colloquial phrase they all seemed to use and that she'd found herself mimicking. Confusing, close to "off course." Like she was now, alone in deep space.

"Aster, I need for you to divert remaining power to controls in this sector. Gravity at minimum. You may close down sector two entirely. Please keep communications running and divert remaining power to this cabin. For now, Doctor Leandros logging out."

Lian noticed she was trembling again.

At least the alarms were not screaming anymore. She'd sealed herself away in the starboard communications cabin of *Aldebaran*'s operations deck. Standard protocol--communications hubs were the safest and most ballasted areas of the ship. She had to stay by the comms. She could not go anywhere else—the ship was dead in space. There was nothing out there she needed to see. Not anymore.

Nothing she could bear to see.

She remembered how it had happened in harsh color and surround-sound. Navigating the freezing corridors, bouncing off the walls, her movements incongruously gentled in the low gravity. Low gravity like home. So light, floating the raw horror. Death. All around her, Terrans strewn, pinned under girders, burned or bled out, sprawled halfway through sparking hatch doors.

Just one core process malfunction that lead to all this brokenness...

She rocked in place, closing her eyes and breathing slower, slower, repeating mantras in her mind.

The place of peace and light and calm. Go to the Forever-Light in your mind. Do not let their hell touch you. The place of peace and light and calm...

Something in the air changed. Lian flicked open her outer lids. Small objects hovered in the cabin and she almost smiled in relief. Aster had reduced artificial gravity, just as asked. She stretched her limbs and swayed her tail through the cool air, graceful in her own hide after so long.

Display modules brightened as remaining power flooded to the communications panel and cabin S.I. terminal. Lian moved closer and studied the navigation charts. No new information. Only the same death sentence--The *Aldebaran's* last known position, tiny dots of blue noting the ship light-years from the Fleet proper. Far beyond The Fringe, Terran Consolidated's least patrolled systems. Drifting.

Lian shuddered. The *Aldebaran's* current state of catastrophic damage was baffling. And how she had survived—

Ackerman's voice, high-pitched and mad with terror. His words just as staccato and harsh as the syllables of his ugly name as he shouted at her.

"You did this! If it weren't for your bullshit tech we'd be safe—"

How she'd wanted to make him see that she would never have harmed any one of them. A revered healer amongst her people, she did not harm others unless war necessitated it. Even then her highest mission was always the preservation of life through vaccines and medicines, chemicals and remedies offered to the many species she encountered.

Five days and a smattering of hours ago Ackerman had yelled in hate and Lian finally answered back. She'd roared, she'd hissed. Angry and aching with grief, the War-Words of the Northern clans. He didn't hear. He was already dead, blasted to pieces by the explosion that ripped through the walls while her tough hide deflected shrapnel.

Her scales, the metal counter and her mask--why she was still alive and they were not.

Lian coughed, fighting down bile and trying to shove away the memory. "It is my fault."

Sharing FTL tech with an alien species wasn't her idea. Too risky, she had said, especially not knowing everything she could about their spacecraft, their physiology, even their plans for the new capability.

No, the exchange had been Zenobia's idea and won the favor of the Matriarchs. In the service of their people, of progress, of expansion, of goodwill, of strategic relations.

"Zenobia." She sighed her mate's Terran name, sorrow thick in her voice.

Her own clan Matriarch said it might not be wise to trust a War-Mother like Zenobia with diplomacy, but in the end, the Mah-tothi-fassiss Council chose them both as envoys—two disparate factions, science and strength.

The mission was simple. Offer sustainable hyperspeed travel and materials for prototypes in a bid to join Terran Consolidated's exploratory fleet reserves, to sit on their council and play at politics and Terran galactic diplomacy.

The *Aldebaran* was the shining new experimental Terran triumph, bound for deep space to make history, propelling the Terrans further than they'd ever been.

Three years of preparation had barely seemed enough for such a project.

It wasn't enough.

Now Ackerman was a stain on the wall of Biomed Lab 3. A harsh man who had cursed her as he died.

But he did not deserve to die. None of them deserved this.

All of them, gone. Empty vessels. The technician who had explained the concept of hell to Lian and laughed it away. The engineers and navigators, the workers who prepared rations and monitored the ship's water supply. The stern, always-serious captain, hidden away in her cabin poring over mission reports.

Zenobia, toiling in the engine rooms. Her partner, her life-mate.

That name is not who she was.

Zenobia, "She Who Most Vigilantly Protects The Daughters Of The Sun With Her Steadfast Strength, The Lights Of Her Soul And Of Her Mind And The Truth And The Heft Of Her Steel."

I shouldn't be alive.

Lian stood abruptly. The pressure at her barely-scabbed wounds, the dull and rhythmic pain of blood pounding through bruise-weakened flesh made her woozy. She tripped, launched across the room and crashed into the wall.

The metallic crack gave way to the sound of rushing air.

"No."

Lian grabbed onto a panel to stop herself.

"Oh, no. No."

The locker's edge had caught on her uniform, bashing into her helm and air delivery system. She looked down. The monitor strapped to her wrist reported heavy damage. She reached around, trying to access the faulty mechanisms and the ruptured intake valve.

She knew there was nothing she could do.

Lian gazed through the clear visor that covered her face, enclosing her in a safety zone of breathable air. Mah-tothi-fassiss were unaccustomed to the high amount of oxygen the Terrans needed to survive. She'd come to accept the helm through the years, its lightweight plastic tubes sighing out a cool, chemical-tinged life-breath that kept her equilibrium in check and her organs functioning at capacity.

Air that was meant to mimic the vermillion skies of her home.

Her clumsiness had cost her. The blurred numbers blinking from the indicator at her wrist were not encouraging. Lian forced her breath to shallow, her hearts to beat slower. She could live for a while if she was meticulous.

An hour. Perhaps two if she did not exert herself.

She moved as slowly as she could across the room and logged back into Aster's emergency program.

"Welcome back, Dr. Leandros. Your air supply is depleting rapidly," Aster warned. "State your request in as few words as possible so that you can preserve your resources."

"Where is...more?" Lian felt strange speaking so abruptly. Shimmers floated in her peripheral vision. Lights like fireflies or embers sparking over a flame.

Slower. Breathe slower.

"Your air reserves are located in each sector hub and a master store in sector two, aft port storage locker. The only area accessible to my systems is the aft deck supply area. Shall I attempt to reactivate power in that sector?"

Lian considered.

What would I be walking into? A leaking air delivery system, my only weapon a stunner. I am injured. I am weakened by a factor beyond anything I am accustomed to.

Aster prompted her again. "If it would assist you in your decision, the port aft locker is located in an area that at last check registered nearly 20% less structural damage than the areas around it that were still online. All systems remain critical but there is a slight probability you may succeed."

Lian still didn't reply.

Slower breath. Gentle heart. Focus on the light in your mind. Focus on the light.

"Going now," Lian said shortly.

"As you wish, Dr. Leandros. I will reactivate power and basic environmentals in the port aft storage locker. Comms and S.I. terminals in the vicinity may be damaged. Exercise extreme caution. I will release the hatch on your command."

Lian nodded in answer though Aster would not see her assertion. She needed supplies. An oversuit, a light source. She inched across the room, using her tail as a rudder to steady her. Lian bumped lightly into the emergency provisions cache, exhausted from the effort and pried it open, careful not to use too much air. Inside she found a baggy environmental hazard suit. Field rations, packets of water.

She'd not yet thought to eat. She laughed then stopped herself.

Breathe...slowly.

She unfolded the suit and any remaining urge to laugh died. Small. Terran-sized. No suits for a tall, long-necked and lashlimbed monster like her.

They liked that word, the Terrans--monster.

Fear a cold shock through her gut, Lian pocketed a water pouch and reached for a protein pack. It felt useful. Even if it wasn't...but she needed useful.

She needed to pretend there was a chance.

"Dr. Leandros?" Aster hailed her.

"Yesss?" Lian couldn't keep the hiss from her voice this time. Too tired.

"I took the liberty of diverting some of the ship's remaining power to run a real-time diagnostic on sector two. All systems have failed catastrophically. A hull breach is statistically probable. Air locks are not registering and hatches are disabled. Dr. Leandros, it is inadvisable to leave this cabin."

Lian looked down at the protein pack she was still clutching. The reflective silver wrapper mirrored a distorted view of her own hand.

"I...sssee." Her tongue was heavy and lazy.

"Dr. Leandros, your vitals are unstable. Please secure yourself in a safe place and await emergency medical assistance."

"Nobody is coming!" Lian blinked. She'd shouted, a sibilant shriek in her own language.

"I am sorry, Dr. Leandros. I do not understand your request. My system is calibrated to recognize over 500 Terran dialects but we have not yet catalogued your--"

"Aster," Lian interrupted. "Accessss language databank Xeno-Mah-tothi-fassissss if you can. Pleasssssse." Lian sagged, her legs giving out. Her tail swung and with the lower gravity, eased her fall to nothing but a gentle sinking in mid-air.

It was happening faster than she imagined—the fading of her senses, the slowing of her blood.

I must be injured beyond what I knew.

"Dr. Leandros, you are in luck. Please select a file for me to load."

"You...choossssse."

"As you wish, Dr. Leandros."

Terran narration echoed around her. "The following recording was provided by envoys Lian and Zenobia Leandros for Terran Consolidated Xeno-Outreach. Dr. Lian Leandros notes that what follows is Mah-tothi-fassiss Matriarchs invoking the Forever-Light during a ceremony of the Daughters of the Sun, a coming-of-age for young females. Theirs is a complex language, nuanced and difficult for organisms with close-set teeth and jaw structures common to bipedal Terran omnivores to mimic. The translation will follow on-screen."

Narration faded.

The Matriarchs called out one to the other in cadenced rhythms, a fugal exchange of history and praise and lore and advice and love and war and hope.

Many voices as one voice.
Many hearts as one heart.
Many songs for one people.

Songs of the engineers who built space-faring frigates and piloted precision fighters, of Lore-Mothers who taught in the academies. Songs of those who watched the broodlings while Flight-Mothers departed on the long-night missions that brought their people resources for technological advancement and trade.

Songs of the glories of the Forever-Light. Death and life canticles, songs that lauded the laws of space and time.

Her songs, her people.

Lian whispered with them.

"Dr. Leandros--" Aster started but Lian interrupted her.

"Activate outgoing messssage."

"As you request. System ready for outgoing transmission."

With the last of her strength, Lian dislodged her helm. The heavy air choked her, catching in her lungs.

"Thisss. Is Doctor Lian Leandrosss of The *Aldebaran*. Message over all frequenciessss. I am sssorry. Zzzenobia ssso convinced FTL drive would complement your propulsion sssystem optimally. I had almosssst fixed your pathogen H-9627-X quandary." She paused, hiccupping with grief. "I am ssso ssssory. Forever-Light guide you. Lian, Daughter of the Sssun, ending transsssmission."

"Dr. Leandros, your vital signs are critical. Please stand by for medical assistance."

Lian closed her eyes.

All around her, the vivid colors of sunset.

The Matriarch of the Western Quadrant and the High Commerce Fleet-Mother bantered in the scented air as they cued up schematics for a proposed flagship. Broodlings gathered around them, watching, taking notes, sketching holo-models in the air, their scales bathed in ruby light.

Fireflies clouding, buzzing towards sun-warmed stone sheltering the clan. Everywhere, light. High stars. Tiny lights on delicate, jeweled wings.

Everywhere, light.

A GUIDE FOR LOST SAILORS

ALLISON S. HAR-ZVI

Allison Har-zvi is a graduate of Williams College and a native of New Jersey. She lives in New York City and works in book publishing.

Taurus rears his horned head, the Seven Sisters huddle together, one of them invisible, and Queen Cassiopeia still sits on her throne in the sky, spending half the night upside down as punishment for once being too boastful. I know they do, still, even down here, where I haven't seen them in God knows how long. I know too that my dear Orion still stands proud and maybe, sometimes, he thinks of me.

Like Cassiopeia, I am being punished, and I have all the rest of my days, it seems, to contemplate my failure. Unlike the queen, I will do so unseen and uncelebrated, and unlike her, I will disintegrate and be lost one day. Men have paid with their lives for my negligence; my punishment is a comparatively small price.

I have lost many things over the years, forgotten so much that is probably of vital importance, but I can still remember the carpenter who made me, a bespectacled man with a penchant for storytelling and the biggest hands you've ever seen. He liked to speak to his projects, for he knew we spoke back to him in our own way, and it must have been he who first told me that the sailors would be counting on me, believing in my power. I was to bring good luck to the voyages, keep my men safe and bring them home whole, to shelter them from storms and serve as a guide and a comfort to them when they were lost. He told me it was because I had a spirit in me; I've never known if he meant there was a ghost or demon or fairy trapped inside me, or if he just meant I had a strong personality.

I do remember vividly the day he told me where I was going. It was an oppressively hot summer day, and the sawdust mixed with his sweat. He wiped his forehead with his hand, which didn't help much, and then suddenly he clapped me on the shoulder. I was nearly there, he said. Once I was completed, I was to be mounted on the prow of a trading ship called the *Opulentia*.

The carpenter did the ship's name proud. He gave me a gilded crown and wreath at my throat, an abundance of tumbling curls, a plump mouth, and an enormous bare bosom and ample curves, and so I went through my life accustomed to the stares of men. Even the mild carpenter would good-naturedly give me a light slap where my rump should be as he walked into his workshop in the morning, and later, after I was on the ship, one of the crew who had had too much to drink tried to climb out onto the prow one night to cup a hand around my breast. He lost his grip before he reached me, though, and tumbled overboard. Another crewmember raised the alarm and they somehow managed to haul the poor soaked man back on board, miraculously unharmed. You can imagine the commotion. The captain had him flogged on deck the next day as punishment, but even as the lash came down upon him, I could have sworn he raised his head to wink at me.

I never minded their advances. I learned to enjoy a lewd joke like the best of the sailors, and swear (if only they could hear me) with as much fervor. And if one of them should make a comment about my breasts or a suggestion of what he'd like to do with me, I learned to pout my big lips at him coyly, knowing that the men were under my protection, and their bawdiness was all in good fun.

I even learned to get used to the constant pounding of the waves against my face, though in time it wore away much of my wreath and crown. I miss the feeling these days; it isn't the same to have the sea envelop you until you don't notice as it is to greet the waves head-on, part from them, and come together again even more furiously.

Do not imagine that because my human form ended at the hips where it joined the prow, that that was the extent of my domain. I was part of the ship, and likewise, the entire ship was connected to me. I could feel its every motion, everything that happened on board: tremors in the rigging and ripples in the sails, the creak of the masts, the slow, labored rotations of the ship's wheel, the cold slosh of water as the decks were swabbed. I could see everywhere, and I knew everything as a part of myself. I could see the flogged man wink at me; I could feel cargo shifting in the belly of the ship.

For many years, I served the *Opulentia* well. Business was good, and I brought the ship all the luck I could muster. I did have power, I discovered. I could sense the ship, sense where it was weak and will those parts to brace themselves against a storm. I could feel when we drifted ever so slightly off course, and influence the ship to steady and not stray. I could sense an argument brewing between members of the crew and help their tempers to ease, or, if not, I could cause small, insignificant accidents for them to deal with, to distract them from quarreling. I cannot say how I know that it was I who did these things, only that I felt something shift as I urged the pieces of the ship to fall neatly into place, the mechanisms to run smoothly, the course to stay true.

I enjoyed the time we spent at anchor as much as the time we spent at sea, watching the people scurrying about on land, so much more diverse and unusual than the crew I had become accustomed to, and so varied, even, from harbor to harbor. I listened to them haggle, gossip, and argue in many languages, exchange many kinds of currency, and sometimes dance and celebrate and tell stories of all sorts. While the sailors took their leave, I listened, and learned what I could.

One autumn, we were anchored in port, a child onshore pointed and tugged at her father's coat, asking about me, who I was, where I had come from, what I was doing there.

He thought for a minute, and, grinning, said, "She was once a common woman who took a job working as a ship's figurehead. But the shipbuilder whose job it was to mount her on the front of the ship fell madly in love with her. He gave her a pretty crown and a wreath and, as a token of his love, stored his own heart on board with her, knowing she would keep it safe."

"And then what happened?"

"Well, as these things sometimes go, she wound up falling in love with the captain a month into the voyage. She let the shipbuilder's heart fall overboard and sink to the bottom of the sea. The ship has had nothing but good fortune ever since, but somewhere, that shipbuilder roams the world alone, doomed forever to remain a heartless man!" He waggled his fingers at her, and she shrieked happily.

No one else was on board at the time to hear the story, but I listened appreciatively. The man was a talented storyteller, to have come up with the idea so quickly, and he spoke to his daughter with such enthusiasm that I sailed away almost believing his story myself.

Those were the good years. We passed across oceans, sometimes as though we were flying. People pointed and cheered to see us pull into port with our cargo. And I continued to do my best to bring good luck to the ship and all on board, because, I found, the sailors really did have faith that I would.

One winter, early on, we encountered a terrible storm. The men were on deck shouting and grunting and pushing and pulling, and I was straining too, trying with all my might to feel around, seek out the bits that were coming loose, the direction we were meant to be pointing, feeling them out, trying with everything I had to right them as well as I could with only my will, as walls and walls of water came slamming down on me.

We made it through that storm intact. It wasn't the first we faced, and it wouldn't be the last, but I remembered that one in particular because of something that happened afterward. We'd made it safely into the harbor, and as the crew disembarked, a cabin boy turned his eyes up to look at me, and smiled.

"Thanks for getting us through that, my girl," he said. "It's good to be home." And as I watched, he raised up his hand and saluted me.

The sailors liked me, and I'd come to feel I belonged with them, but I'd never received so touching a gesture from any of them before. I felt marvelous for weeks afterward, having realized how truly they, or at least this cabin boy, believed in me.

***

While we were at sea, there was activity on board at all hours of the day and night, men joking and singing and working and fighting, and so I could never exactly be what you would call lonely. They were good men, and I was fond of every one of them. Many nights though, there was no one to listen to me in the way I needed. Affectionate though they were, the sailors never learned to quite understand me. That was why, at some point, I started talking to the stars.

They're a spirited bunch, I heard myself say to the sky one night, *But sometimes...*

I didn't have to finish before I felt, in the same way that I could feel the presence of the ship, that something in the stars was listening. And so it began.

I do not remember who it was who taught me the myths about the constellations, only that it happened a long, long time ago. Perhaps the carpenter knew somehow, and told me the stories, once, or maybe I heard them in a harbor somewhere. I do not think it could have been one of the sailors. They knew a great many tales, of course (most of which I enjoyed immensely but would have made a frailer woman blush), but they were not the types to be interested in anything the ancient Greeks might have had to say. They knew all the constellations by heart, but were concerned mainly with using them to calculate latitude and longitude, to find their way among the waves and sometimes to think of home.

Some parts of the sky listened to me better than others, or so it always seemed, and it helped to know that each part had its own story. If I had known nothing about the myths, I might never have come to know Orion, to really know him. I might never even have known that he was a man, let alone a hunter, though I'm sure I would have admired his beauty, even without knowing what he was.

I have spent my life around coarse, burly men, sailors and laborers and hardened, weathered souls. I saw something of them in Orion, though I'd never met a hunter before, unless you count the odd fisherman or whaler here and there. That was a comfort, that he was something familiar among the stars which, admittedly, could seem so utterly alien sometimes. But he was *more* than any of the living men I had known. He was attuned to everything. He could hunt anything. Unlike the sailors, he relied on nothing and no one for luck. He was so powerful, and so very independent, it seemed. And yet I also sensed that somehow he wasn't.

He was different not only from the men I'd met but also from the other constellations as well, so that I found myself longing to speak to him in a way I'd never wanted with any of the others. He was the boldest I'd ever seen, so prominent, so proud, his body straight and square, his belt teasingly askew, bisecting him brightly.

150

I am not a timid one, lord knows. I've spent too much time around sailors for that. But even so, it took me what must have been an age to get up the courage to speak to him.

You're like me, aren't you? I whispered, worried that perhaps I was being too forward. *You've been fixed in place by someone, and steered around without a say in where you go. But people count on you to be where you are.*

A cloud passed over the star that was his right shoulder, so he seemed to half-shrug, but I could tell that he agreed. I know what it means to have limited means of communication, and so I am perceptive when it comes to these things; I knew how to understand him. I grew bolder after that, and soon I was pouring out secrets of the ship, confiding wishes. It wasn't long before I began talking to him every night.

It pains me to remember that that's when the trouble must have started, for the more time I spent mapping out the sky in my own way, the less time I spent attuned to the needs of the ship. I was falling in love with the hunter, but I'm certain that on those nights I spoke to him, if I had paused to listen, I would have sensed the evidence of my neglect, I would have noticed certain elements of the ship's little world starting to go ever so slightly awry.

A minor fire broke out in the mess, but the cook put it out quickly before it could do any real damage. A number of thefts took place on board, and a cabin boy was wrongly accused and whipped. I took no notice of any of it. I was gazing upward.

Orion played hide-and seek with me behind the clouds, some nights. When he was dimmer, I asked what was bothering him, though I usually couldn't discern the answer, even perceptive as I was. When he was at his brightest, I rejoiced. Sometimes I sang to him, songs I had learned from the sailors.

A poorly-tied knot in the rigging went unnoticed until it

came loose while one of the crew was holding onto it, and he plummeted down onto the deck, breaking both his legs but thankfully not his neck. I barely registered the sound he made when he fell.

Of course, Orion was only in the sky during the autumn and winter months, and when he was away, I kept myself busy. I'm sad to say that by then I had fallen into bad habits, had grown addicted to the skies, and even when he wasn't around, I was careless about the ship. Instead, sometimes I tried to strike up a friendship with Sagittarius, or made an effort to talk to the Gemini, though I have always found them somewhat tiresome. I did my best to remain on peaceful terms with the scorpion who had killed Orion, who had been placed on the opposite end of the sky to avoid any further bloodshed. All the time, my crew labored and shouted and sang to pass the time, and I waited anxiously for winter to return.

Around the time of my second winter with Orion, we had a new captain aboard the *Opulentia*, and he made himself almost immediately unpopular. Even I could see how terribly inept he was, and he had a habit of refusing to be proven wrong, no matter what. He periodically took it upon himself to discipline the crew harshly, far too harshly, so that the most minor infractions were dealt with as though they were matters of fatal importance, and then he would slide into long stretches during which he seemed to give up on discipline altogether. He bungled even the simplest tasks, on many occasions. It was no help that at the same time, we had a sudden outbreak of typhus on board.

I should have heard the grumbling on board, felt the tension, the tempers beginning to run high. I should have felt that something was off, and worked to correct it. And failing that, I should at least have seen the sickness and the injustice there on the surface, which anyone with half a brain would have noticed. But I didn't. By that time I was somewhere else entirely.

***

The constellations, I'm certain, are proud of their own myths, even those that end in punishment. They're proud to have a story, proud to have everyone know they were immortalized by the gods, and why. They are, overall, a proud bunch. Perhaps that's what I always liked about them. And I was only too happy to learn their stories, to see them more clearly. Every myth I knew brought me closer to the sky.

One very clear night, the waves calm and the crew quiet, I told my beloved that I had my own myth, too. I told him the story, the story of a man who lost his heart and the ship that carried it away, the story a father had invented about me to please a little girl. It was a simple story of humble origins, and not even a real one, but still it was my own myth, and so I could think of nothing more intimate, more precious, that I could have offered him.

It isn't true, though, I said to him when I had finished retelling it. *The carpenter was a kind man, a good man, and he was fond of me, but we were never in love. And I don't love the captain, either. I only love you.*

It was the first time I had ever told him that, and from the way he sparkled, I could see that he was pleased.

***

Yes, I loved him. I spent a week daydreaming after that. I loved him, and I was an utter fool, so ignorant that I didn't sense the disaster coming until one of the crew told me about it directly.

I was staring dreamily out across the water when he approached. He'd clearly been drinking, and at first I thought he'd try to climb out and reach for me, like the sailor who had once fallen overboard. But he merely staggered over to the side, leaned there, and looked at me with bleary, unfocused eyes.

"'S all set now," he slurred. "We had...a secret meeting. Tomorrow night we're rid of the bastard." He stumbled forward, and righted himself. "Y' won't tell him, girlie, will you? 'Course not. So tomorrow, we take the ship, and the bastard captain..." He bared a set of yellow teeth. "Later we can say the fever took him."

It was only then that I came to my senses, looked around, and discovered just how horribly wrong everything was aboard the ship. We were off-course, the crew was seething, and with a sickening feeling, I realized it had gone too far for me to be able to work any of my little tricks, too far for me to do anything, anything at all.

And so it happened as he said. In the middle of the night, the crew armed themselves. They broke into the captain's cabin and dragged him out, bleary-eyed. They set about taking over the ship.

If I had thought of it, perhaps I could at least have done something to make the mutiny succeed more smoothly, so that we could have made it safely to dry land. But, seeing the chaos, I panicked, I tried frantically to fix every tiny problem I spotted at the last minute, and I suspect I only made things worse. I caused small obstacles to fall in the way of the mutineers as they made their way around the ship, to impede them; it only made them angrier. I tried to bolster the courage of those who opposed the mutiny; they were beaten or tied up or laughed at, and one was killed. I thought perhaps some rough waves or a deviation from our course would serve to distract the crew from their madness and force them to focus on the good of the ship; they paid no mind, and we only spun further out of control.

They couldn't agree on what to do with the captain. Some

wanted to put him adrift on a raft, others thought he should be killed without further thought. In the end they decided to lock him up, and in a last attempt to make the mutiny falter, I tried to make it harder for them to find a place to imprison him. They couldn't locate keys, or found that there was no space, and in the end, in an act of complete idiocy, they chose to lock him in the cargo hold. I should have seen it, though by that point everything was out of my control. It so happened that on that voyage we were transporting, among other things, several kegs of gunpowder.

The captain had many shortcomings, but he was not entirely brainless. He knew how unlikely it was that the crew would let him live. In the end, I suppose he turned out to be made of stronger stuff than any of us expected. Without troubling to light a flame, he stumbled around in the dark, fearful but determined, until, with his hands, he found where the kegs were stored. It did not take him long to make up his mind.

The first mate, far enough from the explosion to survive it, shouted a warning as though he thought it would help, but the fire spread quickly and he was too late. The smoke blocked out the sky.

Oh yes, I always felt the ship's every motion: the pounding of steps on the deck, the groan of the berths as the men who weren't on watch tossed in their sleep, the echo of voices. When the ship split, and the main mast tumbled I felt every moment of the splintering and burning and every last breath that was drawn. I felt the wood crumbling to ash in places and the remaining parts tipping nauseatingly, and a tremendous force sucking us downward, and the bodies sliding over the planks.

***

Time does not pass on the bottom of the sea, except in increments of decay. I have seen the bodies of men become

155

scatterings of bone, and the bones become overgrown with green-brown scum, and the scum eaten off by whatever creatures are willing to venture down this far. I don't know how much is left of me, whether I have any semblance of a face or whether anyone would recognize me as one who was once supposed to watch over a ship, who was meant to serve as a guide for lost sailors, and who so devastatingly failed in the end.

You may say that the mutiny was the crew's fault, not mine. You may say that the captain was the one who set off the explosion, not I. The fact remains that they believed I would bring them in to port safely, and I did not. I could have found a way, I don't doubt it, to ease their disputes if only I had seen the trouble in time, but I was too focused on a love farther away, a love that could never be anything more than stolen whispers in the night.

And the worst of it? I haven't atoned. I hardly ever think of the crew, though their bones lie before me. I have forgotten how their songs go, their faces have faded, and my memories of them seem like something from another life: the drunk man who fell from the prow trying to reach me, the cabin boy who thanked me at the end of a stormy voyage, the last captain's bumbling attempts to keep order, a midshipman who played a wooden flute, a first mate who liked to whittle whenever he had a spare moment. I do not mourn them as I should. No, in spite of everything, I still mourn only the loss of Orion, who I have not seen in so long, who I can still picture, every point, every feature, as though he were here with me on the seafloor. And so I fail my men yet again, and so I rot.

Beneath the ocean, the underside of the surface billows like a blanket and everything is silent. The water wears away at you so slowly that you don't even feel it, most of the time. Time does not pass, and so I cannot say how long I've lain here, how long before now, as something large breaks the surface above.

Suddenly, I find myself bound up by heavy cords. With a terrible gurgling crunch, I feel myself separate forever from what is left of the ship, a sharpness and then a deadness where once there was a presence, however decayed. There's a distant shout of voices, and they must have come for the ship. Someone has discovered me.

Whoever they are, I don't know whether they'll see fit to save me, slap on a fresh coat of paint and carve me back into place, or whether they'll just see an old, weathered piece of wood to be tossed onto the fire. You know, I won't mind. I'll blaze in brilliant, unexpected colors if they do, and maybe they'll clap, holler, sing and tell stories, their children will gasp in amazement, and they'll talk about that night for years to come.

The cords groan and I am rising, up, up, abandoning the bones of the crew for the final time. I am rising, the stifling sea blanket growing nearer, and when I break through it there will be one less barrier between me and the sky. If I burn, I'll rise higher still, the smoke carrying me upward through everything, and, the carpenter's work undone, I'll make my way, formless, through the air, to blow and drift where I will, at last.

ABOUT THE COVER

URSULA K. LE GUIN

Ursula Kroeber Le Guin was born in 1929 in Berkeley, and lives in Portland, Oregon. As of 2013, she has published twenty-one novels, eleven volumes of short stories, four collections of essays, twelve books for children, six volumes of poetry and four of translation, and has received many honors and awards including Hugo, Nebula, National Book Award, PEN-Malamud.

First published in the 1960s, her work has often depicted futuristic or imaginary alternative worlds in politics, natural environment, gender, religion, sexuality and ethnography.

ERIN DEMOSS

Erin is a graphic designer from Oklahoma who geeks out over typography and information design. She has been interested in art all her life and fell in love with graphic design and illustration while going to school for public relations. She is a cat lady, a Leo, and a Star Wars nut. Her favorite book is American Gods by Neil Gaiman and her spirit animal is Louise Belcher.

Want to help us keep growing, support women authors, and bring great stories into the world?

You can buy an issue in print or digital, donate directly, or simply spread the word about Luna Station Quarterly and the wonderful women writers, columnists and reviewers that make up our vibrant, creative community!

FIND OUT MORE:
lunastationquarterly.com/support-us

www.ingramcontent.com/pod-product-compliance
Lightning Source LLC
Chambersburg PA
CBHW070928130626
46555CB00001B/333